"I have a daughter to protect," Paula defended the blunt edge of her tongue. "To think I was willing to talk to you about visitation. You can forget it now, not after this!"

"Listen!" Colt cut in, gripping her arm. Paula froze. But the distant wail was sirens, not armed men returning.

Colt slipped a postcard inside an envelope and moved with a limping gait toward the back door.

Paula's jaw dropped. "Aren't you going to talk to the police?"

He kept moving.

"Go on, then. Run. It's what you do best. *I'll* wait for the police." And she was left alone with her assailing fears.

What if the police don't believe me? What if they think I broke in and made this mess? What if they arrest me? Dear God, what am I doing here?

Books by Susan Kirby

Love Inspired

Your Dream and Mine #64
Love Sign #129
Love Knot #253

SUSAN KIRBY

has written numerous novels for children, teens and adults. She is a recipient of the Child Study Children's Book Committee Award, and has received honors from the Friends of American Writers. Her Main Street series for children, a collection of books that follow one family through four generations of living along the famed highway Route 66, has enjoyed popularity with children and adults alike. With a number of historical novels to her credit, Susan enjoys intermingling writing-and-research travels with visits to classrooms across the country.

LOVE KNOT

SUSAN KIRBY

Love Inspired

Published by Steeple Hill Books™

STEEPLE HILL BOOKS

Steeple
Hill®

ISBN 0-373-87263-1

LOVE KNOT

Copyright © 2004 by Susan Kirby

All rights reserved. Except for use in any review, the reproduction
or utilization of this work in whole or in part in any form by any
electronic, mechanical or other means, now known or hereafter
invented, including xerography, photocopying and recording, or in
any information storage or retrieval system, is forbidden without
the written permission of the editorial office, Steeple Hill Books,
233 Broadway, New York, NY 10279 U.S.A.

All characters in this book have no existence outside the imagination of
the author and have no relation whatsoever to anyone bearing the same
name or names. They are not even distantly inspired by any individual
known or unknown to the author, and all incidents are pure invention.

This edition published by arrangement with Steeple Hill Books.

® and TM are trademarks of Steeple Hill Books, used under license.
Trademarks indicated with ® are registered in the United States Patent
and Trademark Office, the Canadian Trade Marks Office and in other
countries.

www.SteepleHill.com

Printed in U.S.A.

For this reason a man will leave his father and mother and be united to his wife, and the two will become one flesh. This is a profound mystery— but I am talking about Christ and the church.

—*Ephesians* 5:31-32

Kolton Levi and Nicholas Alonzo Kirby
Loving
Anticipating
"…in a flash, in the twinkling of an eye,
at the last trumpet."

Chapter One

Jackson Sign Company was headquartered in the little farming community of Liberty Flats, Illinois, behind the home of Kate Grisham. Kate's granddaughter, Paula Jackson Blake, co-owned the business with her brother Jake. She and Jake and her sisters were throwing a garden party for Gram Kate's birthday. Friends and family visited in cozy clusters on the sweeping lawn and deep porches of Gram's inviting arts-and-crafts home. But in the kitchen where Paula was chastising her daughter Joy, the mood was anything but festive.

Joy's sullen demeanor heightened Paula's concern over the widening gulf between herself and her preteen daughter. At issue this time was Joy's transgression against Shelby, who had driven down from Chicago to attend the party for Gram Kate. Jake intended to ask Shelby to marry him. A close-knit family, Paula and her sisters, their husbands and children—everyone in the Jackson clan—were holding their collective breath on Jake's behalf.

With the exception of Joy.

"You liked her at first," reasoned Paula. "If you would give her a chance, I'm sure you could like her again."

"The way you're giving Dad a second chance?" returned Joy.

"This isn't about your father," Paula reasoned with studied patience. "We're talking about you hacking into Shelby's story. You invaded her privacy and you put Jake in a difficult position. He deserves better. Why, he's like a father to you."

"Uncle Jake wouldn't have to play father if you'd just told Dad about me in the first place. When are you going to get over it and let my dad be a *real* dad?" Joy cried as she fled the room.

Paula might have gone after her if not for her

friend, Antoinette Penn. "Easy does it, she'll come to her senses," Annie said soothingly.

"I've taken leave of mine, letting her talk to me like that," muttered Paula. "That's twice she's wreaked havoc on that computer. First with Colt and now this. And right under my nose!"

"You're not blaming yourself, surely. Who'd dream she'd sneak a peek at Shelby's writing much less track down her father without leaving home?" Annie wagged her head. "It's off the subject, but I can't help thinking what a shock it must have been to the man to learn he had a twelve-year-old daughter."

"*Shock* is a positive pregnancy test, and Colt long gone," countered Paula.

After all these years, the void created by her husband Colt having walked out on her before she realized she was pregnant continued to have enormous repercussions. Paula swept dark-auburn hair away from her throbbing temples.

"I know Joy's frustrated by my stalling," she reasoned. "But what if I let her get involved with Colt only to find out he isn't a fit parent?"

"Why wouldn't he be fit?" asked Annie.

Grappling with a shame she didn't want to feel, Paula blurted, "He's homeless, Annie!"

Annie's eyes widened. "No way!"

"It's true," said Paula, though she could hardly believe it herself. "Shelby volunteers at a homeless shelter in Chicago. Jake tagged along to help one afternoon. Colt was there for dinner, and I don't mean to serve it."

"Are we talking about the same Colton Blake? The Voyager?" cried Annie, incredulous.

"Yes, the Voyager!"

It was the name by which the world at large knew Colton Blake. He had begun modeling for Wind, Water and Sky Outdoor Gear several years prior to meeting Paula. The sporting good company's ad campaign depicted him as a rugged outdoorsman clad in denim jeans, flannel shirt and leather boots. But it was the red knit voyager cap he wore that accounted for his now famous moniker. He embodied the unfettered spirit, and not just on billboards and in slick magazine ads.

Wind, Water and Sky Outdoor Gear used that one enduring image of Colt as the centerpiece of their ad campaign. Business had sky rocketed. The company was now a global enterprise. Which made it all the harder to explain how Colt could be reduced to living in a homeless shelter. In response to Annie's questions, Paula could only recount what Jake had learned from the mission director, Mr. Weaver.

"It seems Colt's recovering from an accident."

"What kind of accident?" asked Annie.

"Mr. Weaver didn't say. But Jake said it left him badly scarred."

Annie winced. "That can't be good in his line of work."

"Still, you'd think he'd have a bank account the size of Texas," Paula said, struggling to come to terms with recent events. "So what's he doing convalescing in a homeless shelter? How am I going to protect Joy from that?"

"You can't. You'll have to tell her," reasoned Annie.

"How, without diminishing Colt in her eyes?" asked Paula. "Don't you see? She'll be devastated. The only way to shield her is to keep her away from him."

"That isn't going to work forever," said Annie.

"It isn't working now!" In the same breath, Paula wailed, "I'd like to take an ax to that computer!"

"Or you could meet with Colt, resolve your issues and move ahead," reasoned Annie, ever the voice of reason.

"Talk face-to-face?" Paula grimaced. "No thanks."

Annie let it go and changed the subject. "Are you busy later? If not, stop by the house and I'll trim your hair."

She could visit with Annie and still be home in time to enjoy her role as hostess to Shelby, who would be spending the night at her house. As for Joy, she was staying the night here at Gram Kate's. "Thanks, Annie. I could use a cut and some conversation," said Paula. "How's seven sound?"

"Perfect. See you then," Annie said, and let herself out.

What with guests to thank and bid goodbye and general party cleanup, afternoon flowed into evening. Paula joined the rest of the Jackson clan around Gram's dining room table for a casual dinner.

When the dishes were done, Paula's sisters

retired to the parlor where Joy was watching old home movies with Gram and various other family members. Paula bussed her cheek good-bye, and was trekking back through the kitchen to leave for Annie's house when the phone rang. The caller was a woman who identified herself as Monique Lockwood and asked to speak with Jake.

"Just a moment please," said Paula.

"I've got it on the portable, Mom. I'll get Uncle Jake." Joy's voice came over the line.

Jake had moved in with Gram months ago when her failing mental health made living alone a hazard. Jake's portable phone hadn't proved all that reliable. With that in mind, Paula kept the connection, waiting for Jake to pick up.

"Hello?" said Jake.

"Mr. Jackson? My name is Monique Lockwood. We met at the mission last weekend. Mr. Weaver gave me your number. He said you had asked about Jig-Saw, and had the impression you might have information concerning him. You *do* know Jig-Saw, don't you?"

Jig-Saw? Paula drew the receiver back to her ear. *Wasn't that the name Jake had said Colt was known by at the mission?*

"Yes, I know him," came Jake's clipped reply.

"I understand how you might be reluctant to pass along information to a stranger. But I'd appreciate it if you would hear me out," said Monique. "Jig-Saw would like to see his daughter, now that he's more fully recovered."

"Recovered?" echoed Jake.

"From his accident. I assumed you knew about that."

Jake offered nothing.

"The bottom line is he's jobless and penniless and trying hard to get back on his feet. In the meantime, he asked if he could use my place as home base. Just for a day, long enough to have a nice visit with his daughter."

Over my dead body! Paula's blood rolled to a boil. Colt had no right to make arrangements behind her back. *Who was this woman, anyway?*

"In your opinion, would I be safe in letting him stay?" the woman unknowingly fanned Paula's ire.

"You're asking me if he's dangerous?" came Jake's even reply.

"Exactly."

"If you don't know him any better than that, why would you consider opening your home to him?" reasoned Jake.

"I've been in desperate straits myself, and received help with no motives beyond simple kindness. You understand?"

"I'm trying to," said Jake. He was silent a moment, then offered guardedly, "The guy I knew wouldn't be a risk to your property or your safety. But it was years ago that I thought I knew him."

"May I ask what your relationship to him was in the past?"

Paula anticipated a straightforward, "He's my brother-in-law." Instead, Jake said, "I'm not free to say."

At that, the woman thanked him for his time and abruptly ended the call. Paula hung up the kitchen phone. She was anxious for a word with Jake. But Gram wandered into the kitchen, agitated over her misplaced crocheting. Paula found it for her, and led her back to the parlor where she learned from Joy that Jake had left the house in search of Shelby.

"Shelby's not with him?" asked Paula. "Where is she, then?"

"I don't know, Mom. She left by herself," said Joy.

Fearing the worst, Paula cried, "Oh, dear! I hope they haven't quarreled. If only you hadn't hacked into her story!"

"Shelby leaves, and you blame me. That's real fair. No wonder I have nightmares," groused Joy. "Where you goin'?"

"To find Jake." Paula paused to offer a quick apology for her hastily drawn conclusion about Joy's part in Shelby's departure. She reeled for the door, adding, "Don't forget the pancake breakfast. I'll call you at six."

Paula drove home. But neither Jake nor Shelby's vehicle was in her drive. The house was dark. Baffled, she circled the town in a fruitless search, then gave up and went to Annie's house where she got a hair cut and some straight talk about getting the facts on Colt, and pronto.

Admiring her feisty friend, Paula sighed. "I should be more like you, Annie."

"Red-haired, you mean?" Annie grinned and reached for a bottle of Miss Clairol in a wordless dare.

It wasn't what Paula meant. Nor could she

explain why she was suddenly taken with the idea. But with a reckless shrug she countered, "Go ahead, Annie. I'm ready for a change."

The results were stunning. Paula left Annie's house feeling fortified for "fact-gathering."

Afterward, Paula drove home to find a note from Shelby. She said she was sorry she hadn't gotten the chance to thank her for her hospitality and say goodbye in person, but that she had decided to return to Chicago a day early. There were no lights on at Gram's. Reluctantly, she decided it would be best to wait until morning to call Jake for feedback on the situation with Shelby as well as that strange phone call from Monique Lockwood.

One thing was sure—she wasn't about to let Colt get away with going behind her back, making plans for Joy to come visit. First order of business was to determine the circumstances that had led to him being homeless.

Paula slept well and phoned Gram Kate's house at six. Gram's sister, Marge, answered the phone. She and her husband Hershel had come for the birthday party, and planned to stay a few days.

After exchanging pleasantries with her, Paula asked to speak to Jake, only to learn he had left in the wee hours for Chicago.

"Apparently he was anxious to iron out a little misunderstanding with Shelby," offered Marge. "I'm glad we were here to be with Kate so he could go. Mercy, but her memory is bad. It just wouldn't be safe to leave her to her own devices."

Paula visited a moment longer, then asked to speak with Joy.

"She hasn't come downstairs yet. I'll wake her and have her call you back," said Aunt Marge.

The phone rang a moment later. It was Aunt Marge, calling to say Joy wasn't there. Thinking she must have left to meet her friends, Paula drove over to the church. But Joy wasn't among the young people who had convened there to prepare a sunrise pancake breakfast.

Alarmed, Paula hurried to Gram Kate's house. Her growing apprehension turned to panic when she found Joy's headphones and a telltale pad of sticky notes by the telephone in Jake's study. The top one bore the inkless impression of a long-distance phone number that matched the last call on caller ID.

Monique Lockwood! Paula dialed the number twice, but got no answer. Heart pounding, she switched on Jake's computer, went online and secured the address from a reverse phone directory site.

Chapter Two

September sunlight streamed through the windows of the white Crown Vic that Paula had purchased secondhand from Gram Kate when Gram gave up driving. The brightness of it caught the fire in Paula's vibrant hair. The hours-old color shift from dark auburn to a spirited red was light-years from her mind as she set out for Chicago. She was twenty minutes from home when her cell phone chirped.

"Paula? It's Jake. I'm in Chicago, at Shelby's apartment. Joy's here."

"At Shelby's? What in the world is she... How did she get there?" cried Paula.

"She caught a ride to Bloomington, took the

bus here and caught a cab. Relax, she's safe and sound,'' he said quickly.

"Thank God! Put her on.'' Relieved tears blinding her, Paula pulled over to the side of the road.

"Now before you go ballistic, keep it mind I was careful. Except for the scary dream I had when I dozed off, it was just a boring old bus ride,'' said Joy before Paula could say a word.

The conversation that followed did little to alleviate Paula's long-term concerns. Joy's intended meeting with Colt hadn't materialized. Terse, willful and frustrated, Joy didn't ask for Paula's help. Or her understanding. Quite the reverse—she was openly defiant.

Jake offered to bring Joy home with him that evening, saving Paula the trip. But Joy's escapade solidified Paula's determination to talk with Colt and determine her next move. She would do it in person, God willing.

Two hours later, with 150 miles of interstate and a maze of traffic-choked Chicago streets behind her, Paula's chest hurt. Her side, too. The pain was sharp, like a runner's stitch. But the marathon was mental. She might have spared herself this day's torment had she tracked Colt down once she learned she was pregnant. But at the time, his abandonment had been one blow too many. She was still reeling from the loss of her parents.

Paula braked for the light at a dreary inner-city intersection, whisked off her dark glasses and double-checked Monique Lockwood's address.

The numbers corresponded with those on a house that had been converted into apartments. It was three doors down from a busy service station. A video store, a mom-and-pop grocery, and a house with tattoo parlor signs in the windows occupied the remaining corners of a junction where commerce and residential collided. Rap music blared from a passing car radio. A pneumatic tire wrench rat-a-tatted. Exhaust fumes poured from an idling car to mingle with clouds of industry and spread a pall over the neighborhood.

The light flashed green. Paula pulled ahead, seeking a parking space. But the curb was full to the end of the next block. She needed gas anyway. Paula circled the block and turned into the service station. But all the pumps were in use.

With a mental note to fill up later, Paula parked out of the way at one end of the station, grabbed her pocketbook off the bench seat and locked her car. Her pale-pink suit with its trim jacket and streamlined skirt hugged fit curves as she made her way around the chain-link fence bordering the station. Wild chicory grew in the wire meshing. Its blossom was as blue as Paula's eyes and as out of place as she on this noisy street.

Her platform sandals hit the pavement, covering the growing racket of an uneasy mind as the distance melted away. Twin wires poked from a hole where a doorbell had once been. Paula curled her fist to match the knot in her stomach and rapped three times. But her prepared speech vaporized as the door swung open, not to the unknown Monique, but to Colt himself.

At point-blank impact, each impression was hard on the heels of another: his black T-shirt, jeans and open tailored jacket, his leanness, his gun-metal gaze, his fingers curling to scratch a short-clipped scalp. Shorter than she remembered, but the same ripe-wheat hair.

Missing was the rugged good looks that had captured Paula's girlish fancy all those years ago. Like varnish that had spilled from a careless brush, scars stood in bold relief, crisscrossing prominent cheeks, proud nose and high brow. As if discerning her shock, Colt's mouth flattened, underscoring his displeasure.

"We need to talk." Paula minced no words.

"If you're looking for Joy, she's not here," he countered.

"I know where she is," replied Paula. "I came to take her home."

"With or without seeing me?" he asked.

"That depends on you. Though you *could* refuse to see her," she added.

Colt's face remained tight, like molded plastic that had buckled in the sun. But those eyes! Lightning struck from their depths. Inquisitive, intelligent, intuitive. Something else, too. Something parental and fierce. It devoured Paula's slim hope that they could come to an agreement that would settle the matter without further trauma or intersecting their separate lives.

She drew a tight, shallow breath before raising her eyes to his again. "May I come in?"

Colt shot a furtive glance over his shoulder. "You've picked a bad time."

"Are you alone?" Paula asked.

"Yes. But I'm in the middle of something. I'll be free shortly."

"I'll wait, then."

"There's a gas station on the corner. Wait there," he said, and would have closed the door in Paula's face except that her quick foot made a barrier. She pushed with both hands to widen the gap, and darted inside.

Thwarted, he said flatly, "You shouldn't be here."

"I wouldn't, if it weren't for Joy," retorted Paula. "Do you want to see her or don't you?"

"I do. But not here. Not now."

"And not behind my back. At least let's agree on that much." Paula laid out what she wanted to hear the same way she had once laid out his clothes.

Colt's jaw tightened. "I had nothing to do with her running away."

"Not directly, perhaps." Yielding to the fierceness of his expression, she gave him the benefit of the doubt, but added, "I'm not leaving until we've talked."

Abruptly, he stepped aside, and closed the door. It was a hollow victory, indicative of nothing. Paula crossed to a well worn sofa and looked back to see him peer toward the street through a crack in the faded curtains. There was a catlike caution, a grimness about him Paula didn't recall from the past. She jumped when he drove home the deadbolt lock.

His limping stride ate up the distance separating them. Paula settled at one end of the sofa. She tugged at her hemline, waiting for him to join her. Instead, he crouched down at the coffee table, and thumbed through a stack of postcards. Photo albums, letters and loose pictures were scattered at his feet.

The circumstances that had brought her to this juncture cycled through Paula's mind. The waiting was like heat under a teakettle, building to a whistling boil. "Are you about done?" she asked at length.

Colt looked up at her, and then at the papers he'd strewn about.

"What am I thinking? You never were much for prioritizing," she said, tension mounting.

"Is that why it took you so long to tell me we have a daughter?" he asked.

"*We* don't, *I* do. And I didn't tell you—*she* did." Paula took issue.

Colt conceded her point with a chilling sweep of gray eyes, and wordlessly returned to the task at hand. Vignettes from the past washed over Paula as she watched his deft right hand flip a scenic postcard and scan the message. Hands that had once caressed and cradled and courted her favor.

Paula slammed the door on her thoughts, and worked instead to fully grasp the reality of the man before her. A man she had once so idolized, now scarred and broken. This was no time for sympathy. He would spurn her pity just as he had spurned the love she had once given.

Paula laced her fingers in her lap and checked the jittery impulse to tap her foot. The silence stretched between them. Again, the tension mounted, expanding like a balloon about to pop. So much so, she jumped when he cleared his throat.

"That should do it." Colt set a single postcard to one side and came to his feet. "I'm free now to hash out visitation arrangements. Where would you like to finish this discussion?"

"Not so fast. I'm a long way from granting rights of any kind." Paula started violently at an erratic popping sound from the street. The glass in the front window exploded from its frame.

In one fluid movement, Colt grabbed the postcard, lunged over the coffee table and drove Paula to the floor. "Keep your head down!" His cry rent the air.

The echoing staccato, the breaking glass, his crushing body went over her in an explosive wave. Even as she shrieked, he was rolling off her, warning, "Keep down! Crawl! Go! Go! Go!"

Even as he prodded her into retreat, it penetrated Paula's fractured mind that the popping sound was gunfire. Colt bulldozed her on hands and knees into the kitchen. He shoved a table in front of the door leading from the living room, then flung open the back door.

"Wait for me!" Paula cried out in terror.

Colt turned back for her. Or so she thought until he ducked into the pantry and disappeared through a rug in the floor. Rather, a trapdoor with a ruglike covering.

"Wait! Don't leave me!" she sobbed.

Colt caught her by the ankles and guided her down after him into the dingy crawl space. Dank air pressed close as he pushed her to one side, then stood on a paint can to reach the pantry door through the open trapdoor. He shut it, then pulled down the trapdoor, closing out all light except a glimmer peeking through a narrow grimy window.

He dropped beside her. "Are you hit?"

Unharmed, and numb with disbelief, she

stammered, "Why would anyone...who would want to...are we going to die?"

"Shh! Get a grip," snapped Colt.

Finding him only a stripe less frightening than the terror above, Paula huddled trapped in a half-standing position in a four-foot-high tangle of plumbing pipes and furnace duct. Claustrophobic, she fought engulfing panic. Horrific bumping and banging above gave way to heavy footsteps and swearing men. The pantry door creaked. The footsteps stopped.

Paula squeezed her eyes shut. She whimpered for air. Stars flickered behind her eyes. Colt clamped a hand to her mouth.

Chapter Three

Paula struggled to be free of Colt's constricting arms. "Let go, I can't breathe!"

"Be still, then!" Colt warned. His jaw scraped her cheek as he tipped his head, listening.

The silence in the crawl space was so deep, Paula's racing heart was deafening to her ears. If not for the iron bands holding her upright, her legs might have melted beneath her as pounding feet and gruff voices rang through the house. Paula's internal sirens screamed as cupboards banged open and drawers crashed to the floor. It seemed like years before the sounds of the frenzied search gave way to fleeing feet. A door slammed. Then silence.

The whisper of contents shifting in Colt's pocket echoed like a shout down a tunnel. Paula fell to her knees on the dank earthen floor. A sob caught in her throat.

"Don't move, not one inch!" Colt's warning echoed in his hushed voice and hard glance. As he moved away from her, Paula huddled in her own embrace. Colt lifted the trapdoor and let himself out.

His stealthy footfalls moved through the apartment one floor above. Once again there was silence. Her ears ached, listening for him. At length, he came back and stood overhead. Gray eyes peered down at her from ridges and valleys of scarred tissue.

"They're gone. Let's get you out of there." He flung the trapdoor into the kitchen.

Paula teetered on a paint can, but was hindered by her slim-fitting skirt.

Colt gripped her beneath the arms and hoisted her up and onto the floor. Paula perched there, with her feet dangling into the crawl space. She dragged trembling fingers through her hair and blinked back threatening tears.

"You missed one." Colt indicated with a fingertip a cobweb still caught in her hair. "What have you done to yourself, anyway?"

"Done?"

"Your hair."

"My *hair?*" blubbered Paula. "P-p-people breaking in! Sh-sh-shooting at us! Ransacking the house! And you ask about my hair?"

"Next time, you'll scram when I tell you to." He gripped her hands and set her unceremoniously on her feet.

"There won't be a next time. Ever!" Paula replied. In the grips of aftershock, she stumbled out of the cramped pantry and into the kitchen where the contents of drawers littered the floor. "What am I s-supposed to t-tell Joy?"

"About what?" asked Colt.

Paula indicated with a wide-flung arm and a tear-dampened hand the chaos leading back to the bullet-riddled wall just beyond the kitchen threshold.

"Forget it. This has nothing to do with her," he said curtly.

"How can it not? She was *that close* to losing us both! And then what?" Paula's fear spilled into anger, an accumulation of moments, months, years. "Look at you! The symbol of American manhood, plastered on billboards all over the country, dodging bullets! Hiding in a rat hole. Reduced to a penniless, homeless…"

"Has-been?" he offered.

"I have a daughter to protect," Paula snapped, defending the blunt edge of her tongue. "To think I was willing to talk about visitation. You can forget it now, not after this!"

"Listen!" he cut in, gripping her arm.

Paula froze. But the distant wail was sirens, not armed men returning.

Colt jerked an empty envelope from a pile of debris, scribbled an address and retrieved a stamp from a booklet in his billfold. He slipped the postcard inside the envelope, sealed it and moved with a limping gait toward the back door.

Paula's jaw dropped. "Aren't you going to talk to the police?"

"Later. It's Monique's house." He shot the clipped explanation over his shoulder as he started away.

"So? We didn't do the damage."

He kept moving. Tears stinging, she balled

her fists and took a parting shot. "Go on, then. Run. It's what you do best. *I'll* wait for the police."

He wheeled around. "You sure you want to do that?"

Paula glowered. Mute. Arms crossed.

"Suit yourself." His gruff words trailed after him as he turned out the door.

Paula watched Colt cross the tired grass with a limping, ground-eating stride. Her eyes leaked in the glaring September sun. She was alone with her shredded confidence and assailing fears.

What if the police don't believe me? What if they think I broke in and made this mess? What if they arrest me? *Dear God, what am I doing here?*

Heaven was silent. Self-preservation battled years of trust in the wrinkle-proof principles of presumed innocence. "Colt? Colton! Wait up." Paula darted out the door.

Colt heard her following, and slowed to let her catch up. "Where's your car?"

"At the service station." Paula fished her keys from her purse. Resuming his stride, Colt stretched out a palm for her keys. Paula withheld them. "What's so urgent it won't wait until we've talked to the police?"

"I need a mailbox." He scanned the service station parking lot. "The white number yours?"

Paula nodded, then swiveled as a police car came shrieking around the corner.

"Easy does it. Just gawk like everyone else," cautioned Colt. Feigning curiosity, he blended in with alarming ease.

A second police car screeched to a stop in front of the rambling apartment house. Two officers spilled out and raced for the house, guns drawn. A third officer warned bystanders to take cover while they secured the area.

Flight flew in the face of everything Paula believed in. Nearing the car, Paula heeded internal sirens and balked. "This is so wrong. Tell me what it's about!" she pleaded.

"No time."

"Condense it, then!" She stopped short, mind set. "I'm not going anywhere with you until you explain."

Colt shoved his hand in his pocket, cocked his head and sighed. "I found a postcard that blows the alibi of a man who was questioned five years ago in connection with a murder and I don't want it falling into the wrong hands. Satisfied?''

"What man?"

"Simon Burwell."

"Who is he?"

"A high-profile Chicago real estate mogul and Monique's ex-husband."

"To *you,* I mean. Who are these people to *you?*" said Paula in quick staccato.

"I'm working undercover on a piece for *Profile Magazine.* This card is key to a story Simon Burwell can't afford to have told. May we go now, please?"

"You're writing again?" Paula's surprise yielded to relief. But only briefly. Not ten feet away was his high-rise depiction, on a Wind, Water and Sky billboard. At a loss to understand how he could be penniless, she blurted out, "I know about the homeless shelter. I'm sorry, I don't want to embarrass you. But Jake saw you there."

"And nearly blew my cover with Monique," muttered Colt.

Cover? Bewildered, Paula shaded her eyes in the sunlight. She looked up at the billboard, and back again. "So what are you saying—you were just *pretending* to be homeless?"

"That's right." Following her glance, Colt said, "Forget all that. It has nothing to do with any of this. C.J. took my place at Wind, Water and Sky years ago."

C.J. was Colt's brother. His name fell like a match over a candle wick. She'd seen pictures of him. He was the spitting image of Colt. Possibilities flickered. "You're no longer modeling? C.J.'s the Voyager? All this time, you've been…"

"Writing," Colt finished for her. "Now that we've clarified I'm still a man of means, could we go, please?"

"Your *means* are of no concern to me beyond how you relate to Joy." Paula climbed behind the wheel. She slammed the car door, and reached for her seat belt as Colt took the passenger seat. "Give the postcard to the police, why don't you?"

"What I write won't be worth the ink to print if the local papers learn of this postcard before the magazine goes to press."

"You have Monique's permission to take it?"

"It's in her best interests that I do. I'm sorry you got caught in the middle of it. But once you barged in, you stuck like a burr."

"I wouldn't have *barged in* if Joy hadn't run away from home, looking for you!" retorted Paula.

"Okay, okay. Simmer down. One crisis at a time." Leaning forward, Colt pointed. "Turn here at the corner, and pull over. There's the drop box."

Paula rolled to a stop at the curb. Colt climbed out and limped across the street to the mailbox.

The sun was in Paula's eyes and the air-conditioning hadn't yet cooled the car. She unbuckled her seat belt and reached into the back seat for the wide-brimmed hat she had donned for church that morning, then pushed thick red tresses up under the crown.

Colt mailed the envelope containing the postcard and crossed back to the car. Once underway again, Paula launched a fresh barrage of questions.

Colt rubbed a scarred temple. "What would you say to a time-out?"

"Oh, you'd like that, I guess. Give me a ride,

help me dodge the police and don't ask any questions.''

"That's some attitude. You've changed." His eyes lingered on her hair.

Paula sniffed and countered, "Which way to the police station?"

He indicated the next corner. "Take a left at the light."

Paula signaled for the turn. The engine sputtered as they rounded the corner. The car kicked and bucked and rolled to a halt at the curb. Paula moaned in frustration and slipped a palm to her forehead.

"Out of gas?" asked Colt.

She blushed at his tone.

"I don't suppose you have a gas can in your trunk?"

"No." Paula reached for her cell phone to call her auto club.

The air conditioner was low on freon. It had yet to overpower the trapped heat in the car. Paula hit the power window, and was scanning her automatic index for the auto club's number when a light-colored sedan pulled out of traffic and parked behind her. The passenger climbed out.

Ear to the phone, Paula belatedly registered Colt's warning. But before she could put up her window, a swarthy man in dark glasses approached the car.

"Need some help?" he asked.

Colt leaned across the seat and answered for her. "Thanks, but no. She's on the phone with her auto club."

The man reached through the lowered window and jerked the hat off Paula's head. "Nice try," he snapped, and grabbed her phone away. He stuffed it in his coat pocket and reached again, saying, "Hand it over, Mrs. Burwell."

Paula shrank from his clutching hands, with a panicky protest. "I'm not Mrs. Burwell. I don't even know her!"

In a fluid movement, Colt was between Paula and her assailant, shielding her with his upper body, crushing her against the seat. "Listen to her. You've got the wrong woman!"

"Shut up and get away from her! Against the door!" With a right-handed pitch, the man tossed the hat into the back seat of the car. His left hand was in his jacket pocket. The fabric bulged, strained by what appeared to be a concealed weapon. Seeing Colt hesitate, he motioned, saying, "Don't play the hero and she won't get hurt. Up against the passenger door. Now!" he added, as Colt hesitated, weighing his options. "Come on, come on! I don't have all day."

At length, Colt grudgingly shifted and came to rest against the passenger door. Without taking his eyes off Colt, the man yanked Paula's car door open.

"Out!" So saying, he jerked her from the car. "We're gonna regroup. Let Simon sort it out."

"Good idea. Better yet, call him." Colt bounded out the passenger's side and circled the car, urging, "Get him on the phone. Ask him if his ex has a birthmark on the arch of her right foot. Kick off your shoe, babe. Show him."

"Back off, Scar-face. I'm not going to warn you again!" So saying, Paula's captor twisted her arm so hard, she squealed.

Colt charged the man, kicked the gun from his hand, and took him to the pavement. Paula fell with them, but rolled clear as her assailant scrambled to retrieve his gun. Colt intervened with pummeling fists. Paula staggered to her feet and booted the gun into the near lane of traffic.

"Help! Help! Police!"

Hands in her hair, Paula shrieked as the muscular goon caught Colt with a mean punch that sent him sprawling. The man pounced on Colt and showed every intention of beating him to a pulp. Traffic in the near lane screeched to a halt. The driver of the lead car slammed on her brakes and reached for a phone. The second lane of traffic stopped, too. A young man jumped out of a pickup truck and into the fray.

"Off-duty officer. Break it up. On your feet, sir." He pulled Paula's assailant off Colt and to his feet. "Spread-eagle. Hands on the hood of the car." A strongly built fellow with a commanding manner, he instructed Paula, "Wait over there out of the street, ma'am, while I get some backup. Are you hurt, sir?" he asked Colt, as he reached for the pager on his belt.

"I'm okay," said Colt.

His lip was bleeding. He wiped his mouth with the back of his hand and said, "We ran out of gas. This guy pulls up behind us and jerks my wife out of the car, says she's going with him.''

"You know him?'' the young man asked Colt.

"No,'' said Colt. "He mistook her for Simon Burwell's wife.''

"*The* Simon Burwell? Burwell real estate?''

"That's right. He and his buddy…''

Colt turned to indicate the driver of the light-colored sedan. As he did so, the car shot into reverse and then sped forward again. Sunday traffic was blocked. The sidewalk was wide open. *Except for Paula. Brushing her skirt. Turning now, blue eyes going wide as the sedan shot up over the curb.*

Colt gave a warning shout and vaulted forward to push Paula out of harm's way. Paula saw the car bulleting toward her. She flung her arms over her face and froze. One moment she teetered on the brink of doom, the next she was tumbling forward, propelled by Colt's out thrust arms.

A sickening thud deadened the air as the on-rushing car struck Colt and tossed him to one side. He came down on a low border of autumn flowers and landed in pine straw. Paula looked on in horror as the pale sedan sped down the walk and away, leaving Colt a long still shadow on the lawn.

Chapter Four

The world froze, a virtual whiteout. No sound. No color. No air as Paula waited, stunned, unable to move. Colt's left leg jutted out at an unnatural angle. *People did not die of broken legs.* The thought flew through her mind. But it seemed a lifetime before Colt stirred. That small movement sent her scrambling to her feet. A sob in her throat, she stumbled the few yards to his right side. What little she knew about simple first aid came into play: "Lie still, Colt! Don't move!"

Colt opened dazed eyes and gazed past her. His expression was so placid, so peaceful, she looked over her shoulder to see what had wrought such an expression. There was nothing to see. He began to struggle.

"You have to lie still! Help's on the way!" Arms splayed, Paula planted her hands on either side of his head to keep him from moving.

A shudder worked through him. His lashes fell, closing her out. A trembling hand muffled Paula's despairing moan. She could see his chest moving. He was still breathing. But the September sunlight couldn't hold back the encroaching darkness of a time before. The screaming tires of the sedan finding asphalt, the sirens of help wailing to the scene faded to the black vortex of a rainy night thirteen years in the past and the head-on collision that shattered Paula's white-picket-fence world. One car carried her parents to their death. The second, moving a little too fast for conditions, was driven by a man who gave and broke vows in heart-jerking succession and went away without warning or explanation. It was the man whose head now rested in her lap.

Paula's eyes filled. *How could there, after all these years, be tears left for him?* She struggled to stem the tide and pull herself together as sirens heralded arriving emergency vehicles. Care was administered to Colt in a calm, professional, painstaking way that made moments stretch like weeks.

Paula couldn't stop shaking. She couldn't stop crying. Dimly she was aware that the young off-duty officer was now joined by uniformed men. It was surreal, the blood, the flashing lights, the EMT's modulated voices dropping like petals into the tumult of her mind. She moved aside as they loaded Colt for transport.

"We don't want him getting agitated. Talk to him, Mrs. Blake." An EMT helped her in after them. "Help him stay calm. Take his hand."

Paula had forgotten what a broad hand it was. But not the shape and texture of his fingers, or the familiarity of them curling around hers. She lowered her face to his with a hushed and urgent, "Dear God, help him!"

Colt stirred, struggling to open his eyes. "Am I dying?"

"Don't say that!" She brushed grass clippings from Colt's scarred jaw, a gesture as spontaneous as hugging a wounded child. "You're in good hands. God's hands."

"I can't get my breath," he rasped.

"Lord, fill his lungs," prayed Paula. "Give him air. Help us, Lord." Her voice broke. Fresh tears splashed on their entwined fingers.

Colt squeezed her hand. "You left the water running…get a washer for that spigot…."

He trailed off. His hand went limp in hers. Paula lifted fear-filled eyes to the middle-aged EMT.

"Fade out on you again?" he said soothingly. "Just keep praying. Don't fold on us now. Hospital's just two minutes away."

Paula saw the color seep from Colt's face until his scarred skin went from ashen to almost transparent. Parted for all these years, only to be brought together for—

She wrested the thought from her mind. Colt's breath came shallow and labored. Time was compressed into an undulating ambulance scream. And then they were there.

Hospital personnel ushered Paula to one side and gave her papers to sign even as Colt was rolled into emergency. Paula didn't impede progress with explanations of their thirteen-year estrangement. She gripped the pen in cold fingers and scanned the rigid print, looking for the dotted line.

A police detective introduced himself as Detective Scott Browning. He said that Paula's assailant, an ex-convict by the name of Hunter Cates, was in custody, but that the hit-and-run driver was still at large.

"Traffic was blocked. The sidewalk was the only escape route. I don't know if the guy just panicked, or if he didn't care who got in the way, just so long as he escaped." Paula gave her account of what had happened.

"If I'd only reacted more quickly! Colt saw me freeze. If it weren't for him…" The knot grew too large for her throat and found release in fresh tears.

Detective Browning gave her time to collect her composure, then asked, "Tell me what you recall about the driver."

"I didn't really see him. He stayed in the car."

"He didn't participate in the fight at all?"

"No, thank God! That thug didn't need any help. I thought he'd kill Colt!" Paula shuddered.

Detective Browning pressed for details. Paula spilled the whole story about being in Monique's apartment with Colt, about the gunfire, hiding beneath the house as the men tramped through, searching, and how she and Colt fled without talking to the police to mail a postcard.

"What postcard?"

Unclear on the details, Paula repeated to the best of her memory what Colt had said about the postcard disproving Burwell's alibi in regard to a murder, the particulars of which she had no clue.

"And your husband mailed it to whom?"

"I don't know, he didn't say."

"But the card belonged to Mrs. Burwell?" asked the detective.

"Burwell, Lockwood, whatever her name is," said Paula.

She repeated Colt's explanation for fleeing the scene, and what little she knew about his assignment for *Profile Magazine.*

"That's all I know," Paula said. "Maybe if you could reach Monique…or Colt's publisher… Someone must be familiar with his assignment."

A physician stepped into the waiting room to say that Colt had multiple injuries, including a bruised lung and that he had lost a good deal of blood from a chest puncture—he had landed on a lot pin protruding from the ground. His left leg, which had not healed properly from a previous break, needed immediate attention. Dimly, Paula heard him say that he would take bone from another part of Colt's body in hopes that it would reknit itself and mend properly this time, correcting his limp.

Detective Browning accompanied Paula to the surgical wing, then gave her his pager number should she remember anything else that might be helpful.

"We retrieved this from Cates." Detective Browning withdrew Paula's cell phone from his pocket.

Paula thanked him, and when he had gone, tried to call Jake at Shelby's apartment. But the battery was dead. She found a pay phone, got in touch with Jake, explained what had happened and asked him to pick up her car from the garage where it had been towed.

"You want me to bring Joy to the hospital?" Jake offered.

"No, not yet. They're taking him into surgery now. His left leg is broken, his chest is punctured and he has lung injuries. I don't know how long they'll be."

"I'll drop your car by, and wait with you," offered Jake.

"That's not necessary," Paula protested out of a sense of indebtedness to Jake, who was always there when she needed someone to lean on. "Just take my car to Shelby's. Break the news to Joy. Tell her I'll call as soon as I know more."

"You don't have to stay. You don't owe the guy a thing," Jake reasoned.

"I know," Paula sniffed.

"So why are you crying?"

"Emotional whiplash. My eyes started dripping this morning when I realized Joy was missing, and I can't seem to get them to stop. I'm out of change, I have to go."

Paula retreated to the rest room to wash her aching eyes. Her suit was wrinkled and smudged. The knees of her nylons were shredded. And her hair was riotous. She tamed her flaming tresses, peeled off her ruined hosiery and smoothed her clothes as best she could, giving thanks all the while for Jake.

Over the years, as she raised Joy and shared the family sign business, Jake was her safety net. Now Shelby was the light of his life. There was no reason for him to come to the hospital and await word on the condition of a man the Jackson family had written off a long time ago. Herself included.

Or at least she thought she had. Tears welled. *Take the fear. Take the confusion. Oh God, hold my hand.*

The plea brought to mind a favorite hymn, which had been penned by the songwriter in the shadow of death. For the believer, death *was* just a shadow. Her hope in the living light that lay beyond the shadows had comforted her greatly following the loss of her devout parents. Joy had recently accused her of blaming Colt for their deaths. That wasn't true. Shamed by the extremes it took to stir her to pray *for* Colt, and not just *about* him and the brokenness he had left behind, Paula found her way to the hospital chapel. The words of the ministering hand-holding lyrics flowed from her heart and mind, a prayer to the throne of God.

Visiting hours came and went as soft-footed as the handful of people who slipped in and out of the hushed chapel. Petition gave way to simple worship.

A hospital volunteer sought her out to say

that Colt's surgeon would meet her in the lounge adjoining the intensive care unit. Once there, Paula learned from Dr. Sandrelli that Colt had come through surgery well. He would spend a few hours in ICU where he could be closely monitored.

"He's going to make it, then?" Paula asked.

"Barring unforeseen circumstances, yes, I expect him to make a full recovery. Better than new, provided the leg surgery is successful," replied Dr. Sandrelli. "Come, you can see him a moment."

He ushered Paula into intensive care and to Colt's bedside. One glimpse, and Paula's eyes filled again. Colt's leg was wrapped, braced and elevated. The top of his hospital gown was folded forward at the waist, exposing a bandaged chest. As she absorbed the bruises and scrapes and cuts and tubes and monitors recording she wasn't sure what, there rose from the dust of crucified memory a specter of a golden-haired, gray-eyed handsome young man who had life by the tail.

Paula had been a senior in high school, working part-time for the family sign business and saving for college when Colt showed up in Liberty Flats, asking questions about a recent train derailment and a resulting chemical spill, the cleanup of which created a controversy.

Dr. Sandrelli lifted one of Colt's eyelids. Looking on, Paula recalled in vivid detail the light dancing in those same gray eyes the morning she stepped out on the front porch in response to the bell. She remembered, too, her astonishment and how she had gawked and blurted, "The Voyager! I'm gonna faint."

She didn't. But she did have a hard time understanding why a rising star in the advertising world would want to moonlight as a freelance writer.

From that moment forward, she was captivated by the romantic fantasy of Colt stepping down off his billboard to rescue her from a commonplace future with her family's struggling business in their sleepy little farming community.

In those bygone days, Paula was as headstrong as Joy ever thought of being. She ignored the cautionary counsel of her parents to rest on the decision and give the relationship time to grow before committing herself to Colt for life. She skipped college, and on the heels

of a whirlwind romance wed the prince of billboard and moved with him to Chicago. But her
expectations of an idyllic marriage ended on the
dark rainy night that she lost both her parents.

Ironically, the mundane life, the town she
had been so eager to escape turned out to be
the catch net when the three people she loved
most were abruptly gone, one by choice.

Why had he left?

She had an illogical impulse to touch Colt's
cheek, as if the mystery lay in unraveling the
maze of scars. She fought it, hands clenched at
her sides, and backed away.

The doctor took it as a cue. He ushered her
out of ICU and patted her shoulder. "He's
heavily sedated. Why don't you go home and
get some sleep? I'll leave word that you're to
be called, should he awaken and ask for you."

Paula knew that wouldn't happen, but it was
easier to leave her number than to explain. She
phoned Shelby's apartment, hoping to catch
Jake before he left for the motel where he was
staying the night. But Paula had already missed
him.

"Spend the night here," Shelby invited.

"Are you sure? I hate to impose," hedged Paula.

"Nonsense. It's the least I can do for family."

Family? "So Jake popped the question and you said yes? Oh, Shelby! That's terrific! Jake must be over the moon!" Paula struggled to rise to the occasion on the heels of a day that defied description.

"I hope so. I know I am. I'll tell you all about it when you get here," said Shelby. "Hold on, don't hang up. Joy wants to talk to you."

"Mom?" Joy's anxious voice filled her ears. "How's Dad?"

Paula related Dr. Sandrelli's words as best she could.

"Can I come see him?" Joy pleaded.

"He's sleeping, Joy. Anyway, we need to talk first. What you did was irresponsible and dangerous." Paula took her daughter gently but firmly to task.

"I just wanted to see Dad. What's so wrong about that?" whined Joy.

"It's the way you went about it that was wrong," said Paula.

"I was careful. I sat right behind the bus driver," reasoned Joy. "I didn't talk to any strangers. And when things didn't work out, I looked up Shelby. Nothing bad happened."

"To you. Nothing bad happened to *you*," Paula said quietly.

"It's my fault, isn't it?" Abruptly Joy's self-defense gave way to tears. "Daddy wouldn't be hurt now if I hadn't come looking for him."

"That's not what I meant," protested Paula, stricken by Joy's guilt. "I'll see you in a little bit and we'll talk it over, okay?"

"You're leaving Dad there all by himself?"

"There's nothing more I can do for him. He's getting excellent care," reasoned Paula.

"I wouldn't want to be left at the hospital without any family. Would you?" asked Joy in reproach.

Why was it that lately she could never find the right words to explain herself to Joy? Weary to the bone, Paula's resolve crumbled. "All right, then. If it's important to you, I'll stay."

"Thanks, Mom. I heard Shelby tell you that she and Uncle Jake are getting married," said Joy.

"Yes." Encouraged that Joy should bring it up, she said, "I hope you can be happy for Jake. He's waited a long time for the right woman."

"Shelby's okay, I guess. Did she tell you she gave me her story?"

"The one you hacked into? Oh, Joy! You can't keep it! It wouldn't be right."

"You're not listening, Mom. She couldn't finish it. She wants *me* to. It isn't like I asked," said Joy indignantly.

"That's very gracious of her," began Paula. "But I really think you should return it."

"And say what? That I don't want it? That would be kind of rude, don't you think?" Joy countered.

Head throbbing, Paula felt incapable of further thought. It was no time to be making decisions, anyway. "I'll rest on it. You'd better, too," she added.

"Whatever," said Joy.

"I love you. I'll see you tomorrow."

Paula hung up feeling emotionally tattered. But, there was one positive note—Joy seemed to being getting past her fear of losing her standing with Jake. Or was she simply looking ahead, making room for Colt?

The thought caught Paula off guard. She hadn't consciously made the decision to yield to Colt any rights, paternal or otherwise. What had changed? Nothing, except that he wasn't a homeless derelict. Which in no way recommended him as a father.

At midnight a nurse came with pillows for the handful of people keeping an overnight vigil in ICU's visitor's lounge. Paula tried to shut down the mental treadmill and get some sleep. At length, exhaustion proved her friend. She dozed until morning.

Gritty-eyed and sluggish, Paula made her way to the ladies' room. A long look in a short mirror did little for her intestinal fortitude. She splashed water on her face, tamed her bright hair with a comb and damp fingers and fished through her purse for the toothbrush she had received following her dentist appointment last week.

Upon her return, a nurse beckoned Paula to Colt's bedside. "He had a good night," she said, and pulled a curtain.

It was a token gesture. There was no shutting

out the sterile scents and unnerving sounds of human frailties and electronic wizardry within the glass-and-stainless-steel world of ICU.

Colt's eyes were closed and underscored by bruises. His face was puffy. A shave would be a painstaking process, dodging his scrapes and cuts. His nose was swollen. His split lip was puffy too. Then there was the matter of his leg. But at least his color was better. His slate-gray eyes fluttered open.

Ill at ease with the role thrust upon her just by virtue of having kept the vigil, Paula asked, "How are you feeling?"

"Rough," he said, his voice a husky whisper. "You're here about Joy. Or did we already have that talk?"

"No, it can wait until you're feeling better."

"Did they catch the guy?"

"The driver?" Encouraged by his clarity of thought, Paula said, "No. Not the last I heard."

"Burwell's behind it."

While his mental capabilities seemed unhampered, his voice was a slender thread. Taking care not to bump the bed, Paula leaned closer, straining to catch his soft words: "He wants the card."

"You mean the postcard you mailed? I told Detective Browning about that, and what little else I knew," said Paula.

"Card is on the book cover...graphics cover the postmark. But the original is valuable evidence."

His words faded in and out. Paula wasn't certain she understood him correctly. "Did you say book cover?"

"*Wish You Were Here.* It's a travel book. Parnell Press. Jake's girlfriend edited it."

"You mean Shelby?"

Colt nodded, a barely perceptible motion that dulled his eyes with pain. "She'll have copies. Bring one," he said, his voice down to a thread.

"You *know* Shelby?"

"No."

"I don't understand."

"You will."

Her ear was just inches from his mouth and still, Paula wasn't certain she had heard him correctly. Sandpaper whiskers snagged a loose tendril of her hair. Discomfited, she tucked the red strand behind her ears, and thought once again of Joy.

"I know I said we should work through some

things first. Concerning Joy, I mean. But she's eager to see you, and very worried. It's going to be difficult to put her off. So let me know when you feel up to a visit."

"Right away," he urged in a spent whisper. "Hurry back."

Paula swung around as the curtain was whisked open and the nurse stepped into view.

"Doctor is here to see Mr. Blake." She arched a professional smile in Paula's direction and added kindly, "We'll be moving your husband into a private room shortly and you can have a real visit."

Chapter Five

Doctor Sandrelli traded greetings with Colt. "I see your wife is here," he said. "Did she take my advice and go home last night?"

"Stayed, I think," said Colt, his assumption based on her disheveled appearance. The grace of her concern touched him.

The doctor took note of Colt's clammy brow and fast pulse. He plugged his stethoscope into his ears. "How many years have you been married?"

"Thirteen." Colt kept it simple.

"And she can still get your heart kicking? Bless you, my good man."

Mind your own business. Colt didn't say it.

He closed his eyes and bore the torment, both of his past and of the examination that followed. He was rewarded with a room of his own.

The move exhausted him. He slept awhile and awoke with a lot of stiffness and a lot of pain. But he resisted asking for pain medication. He wanted to be alert when Paula returned with Joy.

It had knocked him for a loop when Joy contacted him early in the summer, claiming to be his daughter. A phone call verified it was so. Overnight, the career that had been his life lost first place. At first, his urgent desire to meet Joy was governed by the guilt he bore concerning Paula. But as time passed and the shock faded, he grew impatient with her delays. Already, Joy's childhood had all but passed him by.

Colt dozed off and dreamed fitfully of searching in vain for his baby girl. When he awakened, he shook off the dream and tried to put personal issues aside. He needed to work through the events of yesterday. As they coalesced in his mind, he reached for the phone. Every muscle, every nerve, every patch of skin protested movement. But he persevered and punched in Monique's number. It rang unanswered.

Colt tried his publisher and longtime friend, Walt Snyder. But Walt was away from his desk, so he left a message.

Next, Colt rang police headquarters and asked for Detective Browning. His strength was waning fast. Browning had trouble hearing him. "I'll stop by the hospital as soon as I can get away," he said.

Colt slept again and didn't awaken until Detective Browning arrived. The police detective began by asking about the driver who had struck him the previous day.

"Male. Average size," said Colt. That was all he could say with certainty. The tinted windshield and the glaring sun had hindered his vision.

"Do you feel he deliberately hit you?" asked Browning.

"I'm not sure."

"What about your wife? Was his intention to strike her with the car?"

Thinking she was Monique? The possibility had occurred to Colt. Uncertain, he said, "What does his accomplice say about it?"

"Hunter Cates isn't talking."

"What about Simon Burwell?" asked Colt.

"We've been unable to locate Mr. Burwell," said Browning. "Nor has his ex-wife come forward. We're watching her house. But so far, no luck. Your wife says you had just come from Monique Burwell's house."

Colt corrected him, saying, "Monique Lockwood. She took her maiden name back after the divorce."

"You're friends, then?"

"Yes."

"What's this about taking a postcard that you found there?"

"If I hadn't, Burwell's thugs would have."

"Why? What was so important about the postcard?"

Colt was summoning breath to explain when Walt Snyder strolled in on the heels of a perfunctory knock. A middle-aged man with a generous girth, a receding hairline and a deep commitment to family and to *Profile Magazine,* Walt regarded Colt with furrowed brow. "You rest. Leave this to me," he ordered.

Walt introduced himself to Detective Browning. "I don't think Colt's up to this yet. If it's all right with you, I think I can explain most of it.'' He offered Browning the envelope containing the postcard Colt had mailed to him the previous day.

Browning read the message side aloud. '''Wish you were here. Love, Simon.''' Looking up, the detective asked, ''So what's the story?''

''For starters, Simon Burwell was a married man engaged in what was at the very least a flirtation when he mailed this card to Monique Lockwood from Yellowstone Lodge. Note the date.'' Walt leaned in and thumbed the five-year-old postmark.

''I take it that's important to sorting out this matter?'' said Browning.

''You bet. An elderly woman by the name of Myrtle Byron was murdered just a few miles from Yellowstone National Park on that date,'' explained Walt. ''Simon and Roberta Burwell were the only ones with anything to gain by the woman's death, since Myrtle was Roberta's aunt, so naturally the police wanted to question them. Roberta was an invalid and in critical condition at the time they questioned Simon. Needing an alibi, Simon claimed he had been at his wife's bedside here in Chicago when Myrtle Byron was murdered. No charges were ever filed. The case went cold.''

"And his wife?''

"Roberta? She slipped into a coma and never recovered.''

"So Burwell inherited the murdered woman's estate?''

"His wife was the heir, but yes, it came to Simon after Roberta died,'' said Walt. "Briefly, he played the grieving widower, then turned around and married young Monique Lockwood.''

"Are you accusing Simon Burwell of murdering his wife *and* her aunt?'' asked Detective Browning.

"According to the coroner's report, Mr. Burwell's wife died of natural causes. As for the aunt, Myrtle Byron, Simon Burwell was in the area when she died. This postcard proves it. So he had both opportunity and motive in relation to her murder.''

"Motive being?''

"Had his wife preceded her aunt in death, Mrs. Byron might have changed her will,'' Walt explained, making his case.

"I see. You know, of course, that what we're talking about here is out of my jurisdiction," said Detective Browning.

"Yes, I know. But there's a link," said Walt. "Burwell's attempts to get his hands on this postcard explain what happened at Monique Lockwood's house yesterday, and Colt's resulting injuries."

Detective Browning stroked his chin, deep in thought. After a moment, he mused, "Pretty careless of Burwell to have sent Monique the card in the first place. Not to mention leaving it in her possession after their divorce."

"My guess is he'd forgotten sending the card until Monique freshened his memory by featuring it on the cover of her travel book," wagered Walt.

"Travel book?" echoed the detective.

"The contents of the book are irrelevant," Colt spoke up.

"It's the cover that counts."

"You're sure Burwell has seen the book?" asked Detective Browning.

"If he saw yesterday's *Tribune*, he has. They gave it a nice review with the cover featured in color," replied Walt.

He went on to praise Colt for having coaxed Monique into relinquishing the postcard so that justice could be served. Then Colt confessed that Monique didn't know he had it.

"You took it without her permission?" Walt's favor abruptly shifted. "What kind of amateur stunt is that?"

Walt's thunder was no less than what Colt expected. *Profile Magazine* was Walt's brain child. He had nursed it from ignoble beginnings into an uncompromisingly honest periodical respected by the general public and literary critics alike. The conversation soon circled back to Monique.

"Anything else I should know about in that book of hers?" asked the detective.

"No further bombshells that I know of. But I'll have a messenger bring a copy over," offered Walt.

"No need," Colt interjected. "Paula's bringing one."

"Paula? *Your* Paula?" Walt all but cracked the paint with his booming voice. His eyes probed Colt's face.

"Joy took the bus to Chicago without Paula's permission. Paula came after her. She looked me up to vent.'' Colt gave an abbreviated account.

"I see," Walt said, and tapped his hat against his thigh. "At least I know to whom we can attribute your lapse in judgment in taking that postcard. Enough said for now," he added, and stretched out his arm to press Colt's hand.

It was that deep-seated kindness in Walt that had long since cemented their friendship. Mentally, emotionally, spiritually, Walt was larger than life. And no wimp in the physical realm, either. His grip was such that Colt nearly relented on his decision to stay off painkillers so he could fully savor his first face-to-face visit with Joy.

Paula phoned Jake at his motel. Learning that he hadn't yet turned in his room key, she took a cab to meet him and stopped along the way to buy a change of clothes.

Jake was waiting for her in the lobby. A lanky, easygoing fellow with eyes the folks in Liberty Flats called "Jackson blue," he accepted Paula's congratulatory hug with a crooked grin. He gave her the charger to his cell phone along with his room key. "Take your time. I'll be in the dining room."

Jake's room was small, but tranquil. Paula put her cell phone on charge and sat with her Bible, recharging her spiritual batteries as well.

Afterward, she stepped into the shower. The spray of steamy water eased the soreness and fatigue from her body. Refreshed, she dried her hair, applied makeup with a light hand, then donned the streamlined hunter-green skirt and matching short sleeved shell and sweater set she had purchased. On her way to meet Jake, she phoned Joy.

"When can I see him?" cried Joy.

"I'm going to get a bite to eat with Jake, then we'll come for you, and I'll take you to the hospital. Colt asked for a book, something Shelby edited. The title is *Wish You Were Here*. See if she has a copy, and if so, ask her if we can borrow it for a few hours."

Paula met Jake in the dining room. When the waiter had come to take their order and gone, they compared notes on the events of the previous day. Paula's cell phone rang. It was her youngest sister, Wendy. She had spoken with Jake earlier, and was anxious for an update. Paula answered her questions as best she could, and asked Wendy to brief the rest of the family.

Paula's sister Christine, who was with Wendy at Gram Kate's chimed in to reassure her that the gap would be filled until Paula and Jake returned and the family could resume their customary schedule of caregiving.

The waiter arrived with breakfast. Paula was finishing a second cup of coffee when Joy called.

"I thought you'd be here by now," Joy complained in Paula's ear. "I've got the book Daddy wants. Hurry, would you?"

Joy had her father's straw-colored hair, and an open-faced snub-nosed cuteness that showed every likelihood of blossoming into beauty. Her size seven sneakers were rushing the path leading from her tender years to young adulthood. Seeing her waiting in front of Shelby's building with a book under her arm and her chin in the air, Paula was caught in a maternal mix of pride and trepidation.

"I'll bring your car around," Jake said, as Paula climbed out. He leaned across the seat and called to Joy, "'Morning, blondie."

"Hi, Uncle Jake." A feeble smile darted across Joy's face. Her blue gaze was guarded as she looked at Paula. "You still mad?"

"I thought we'd covered that."

Joy tugged at her pink and white striped sweater. "I tried to talk to you about Dad, Mom. But you kept putting off a decision. I got tired of waiting."

"I see that, Joy. But I love you too much to make a snap decision. Was a little patience too much to ask of you?"

Joy responded with an injured sniff. They waited in silence for Jake to bring Paula's car around. Joy climbed in, waved to Jake as he climbed out, and didn't look Paula's way again.

Paula knew no words to bring down that chin. Stop-and-go traffic and a construction detour did little toward easing the breach that had steadily widened since the day Paula learned that Joy had contacted Colt behind her back.

"Have you talked to him, Mom?" Joy broke her silence once they reached the hospital.

"Briefly," Paula replied.

"Can I see him right away, then?" she asked, as they entered the busy lobby.

"If it's all right with Dr. Sandrelli. One more thing." Paula sought words to break the news of Colt's scarred demeanor gently. "You should know your dad...Colt isn't... What I'm trying to say is, he's not exactly like what you may think, based on—"

"His scars?" Joy interrupted. "We exchanged pictures soon after I got in touch with him."

"You knew and you didn't tell me?" Paula couldn't keep the exasperation from her voice.

"I might have, except you growl every time I mention his name," groused Joy.

It was a limited view, but close enough to the truth, Paula relented. "I see. Very well, then. I'll try to do better, okay?"

The volunteer at the reception desk tipped her head in silent inquiry at their approach. Paula asked for Colt's room number and was quickly accommodated.

Joy preceded Paula into the elevator. Two flights up and a few steps into the corridor, Joy stopped short and slapped the heel of her hand to her forehead. "I forgot to get him a present."

"There's a gift shop just off the lobby." Paula opened her purse and withdrew some bills, which Joy folded into her pocket.

"Go on, Mom, I can find my way." So saying, Joy hurried back into the elevator.

The doors fanned closed leaving Paula to

continue alone. She scanned room numbers and found Colt's at the end of the hall. Hearing men's voices, Paula slowed her steps and turned into the room. Detective Browning acknowledged her with a quick glance. A gentleman in a business suit had his back to her. Neither he nor Colt saw her in the open door.

"Any idea how I can get in touch with Ms. Lockwood?" Detective Browning was asking Colt.

"Try her e-mail address," Colt suggested and rattled it off.

"Are you worried about Ms. Lockwood's safety?" asked the police detective.

"Beginning to be," Colt conceded.

"Good morning, Mrs. Blake." Detective Browning greeted Paula. The second man, a portly middle-aged fellow, swung around and paused midsentence. Everything about him seemed to hang in the air—his voice, his gesturing hands, even his thinning hair.

"Paula, I presume," he said finally, his voice as cordial as his eyes were curious. "A pleasure to meet you. I'm Walt Snyder, Colt's editor."

"How do you do?" Paula returned his firm grip. She waded through pleasantries made awkward by virtue of her long estrangement from Colt, and inquired the latest news of Detective Browning.

"Cates's lawyer was in this morning, requesting bail be set. So far, we've put him off." Browning added regretfully that the driver of the car was still at large.

"I see you've brought Monique's book. Could we borrow it a moment?" asked Walt Snyder.

"It's Shelby's, I'll need it back," said Paula, with a glance in Colt's direction.

"Yes, of course. Within the hour," promised Snyder. "Could I buy you a cup of coffee, Detective?"

The men left together, closing the door. To this moment, shared danger and the gravity of Colt's injuries had bridged barriers. But the shock had since faded. The urgency, too. The sound of the door closing behind the men punctuated the silence.

Paula stepped up to the bed and broke the ice. "Are you feeling better?"

"Some, though I won't be skipping rope for a while," said Colt. "Joy with you?"

Paula nodded.

Colt's gaze panned from her to the closed door and back again. "So you're what...the scout mouse?"

"I beg your pardon?"

"Scout mouse. If there's crumbs and no cats, she returns with her young."

"Joy backtracked," replied Paula. "Something about a present for the crumb."

Colt choked on a sip of water. Wincing, he clutched his chest and coughed.

Anxious, Paula asked, "Are you okay?"

He nodded.

"Where's it hurt?"

"Everywhere."

"What're you taking?" she asked.

"Liquids, hold the painkillers."

"You can't be serious. You just had surgery!"

He opened his eyes again. "Don't waste your tender spot on me."

Stung, Paula retreated. "Maybe I'll just go and let you and Joy get acquainted alone."

"All right. Before you go, would you mind dialing the phone for me?"

Paula dropped her purse down in a chair and picked up the receiver. "Who are you calling?"

"Monique."

Paula punched buttons as Colt rattled off the phone number.

"No answer," she said. "What is she to you, anyway?"

"There's nothing between us, if that's what you're asking."

"I wasn't."

"I *am* concerned about her, though," he added. "And you, as well, Paula. You should know that Monique's a redhead. Your current shade," he emphasized. "About your age, your size. That accounts for yesterday's confusion."

"I pretty much figured that out," said Paula.

"I'm sorry about jeopardizing your safety. Believe me, Paula, I wouldn't see you hurt for the world."

It wouldn't taken much of a shovel to dig up the past and prove him a liar. Instead, Paula ducked her head and said, "Thanks. I appreciate the thought."

Continuing, Colt filled in the details concerning Monique's ex-husband, Simon Burwell, Simon's previous wife, Roberta and the murder of her Aunt Myrtle. As the story unfolded, Paula saw the importance of the postcard. If

Burwell wasn't involved, why lie about his whereabouts?

"The police offered to tuck us away until Cates's partner is apprehended and Burwell located for questioning," Colt wound to a close.

It had been a long account for a man of swift-waning strength. One word stood out from the others. "'Us?'" echoed Paula.

"With Cates's accomplice on the loose, we could be vulnerable here at the hospital."

"Maybe you are, but *I'm* not," said Paula hastily. "I didn't see anything. I don't know anything."

"You know that and I know that. But it's the driver worrying the police. Walt as well. He's urging us to play it safe and accept their offer."

"Look, I appreciate the warning, and you can thank your editor for his concern. But Joy has school, and I have responsibilities at home," reasoned Paula. "I can't put my life on hold for fear a thug who mistook me for your friend Monique is now nervous that I can pick him out of a lineup. *You* go."

"Not without you." His gray eyes caught and held her startled blue glance.

"Of course you will. You must!" she insisted.

"How would that look? I can hear your family now. 'He always did know how to look after his own skin,'" replied Colt.

Defensive, Paula sniffed and countered, "Since when did 'his skin' get so thin?"

Heat rushed up Colt's neck. "I cost you your parents, Paula. I couldn't live with you then. I can't now. And I sure can't live with myself if something happens to you because of my carelessness."

Again his words kicked the door open to their briefly shared past. Paula's stomach dropped like a stone and splashed tears to her eyes. She turned and nearly collided with Joy in the open door as she left the room.

Not that Joy noticed. She had a gift-wrapped package in one hand, a rose in the other and eyes only for Colt.

Chapter Six

Shaken by how quickly things had gotten out of hand, Colt briefly mistook the pink-and-white clad youngster in the doorway for a hospital volunteer. She had a red rose and a package and a tentative expression that warranted a second glance. Jackson-blue eyes stared back at him.

Her hair was the color of ripe wheat in sunshine, and curled about her face.

Colt's past imploded upon him. He couldn't speak for the knot in his throat as Joy turned a toe in the way his brother C.J. used to do when he got stage fright.

"It's me, Joy." She tilted her head and arched a tottery smile. "Sorry I'm late."

Colt swallowed and beckoned Joy closer. She stopped short of touching his outstretched hand and gave him the rose instead.

"Thank you." Spellbound by fair, freckled skin, bright curly hair and fetching demeanor, Colt said lamely, "You have my hair and your mother's eyes."

"Jackson-blue, I know. This is for you, too," Joy added, and gave him the package.

The paper rustled as Colt stripped it away to reveal a box of chocolates.

"Butter creams. Milk chocolate," she said, eager for his reaction. "I hope you like them."

"My favorite," he said.

"Really? Mine, too!" Her smile warmed as she confided, "Mom can't eat them. She breaks out."

"I know. Hard to court a girl who can't eat chocolate," he said.

"She likes roses, though."

"Yellow ones. I remember," he said.

A faint crease deepened into a dimple as her face caught the sunshine peeping through the half-drawn blinds.

"Do you still love her?"

"Nice manners," remarked Colt.

She lifted one shoulder. "Just thought I'd ask. Because if you do, I can help."

"Help *who?*" he asked.

"You, if you want. If not, I'll help me." Shoulders back, chin squared, Joy dimpled.

"That's what I thought."

"So do you want help?" she pressed for an answer.

"I appreciate your concern, but I think I'll pass," he said.

Joy sighed her disappointment. "Forget I asked then, and open the chocolates."

As Colt passed her the box, he noted that her chin was still up there in the nosebleed section. *Like Paula's, when she dug in her heels.*

Joy also had Paula's gift for gab. Her exuberance was music to his ears. Colt held on to each syllable as long as he could. But eventually, he lost his will to fight the overwhelming weariness. Joy's lilting strains ran together in a soft faded hue. His awareness melted away like the chocolate in his hand as he surrendered to mental and physical exhaustion.

* * *

Paula fled to the ladies' room. She stood with her back to the wall, Colt's words reverberating like thunder: *I couldn't live with you then. I can't now.*

Why? The question remained lodged where it had taken root the morning she tumbled out of bed to find Colt's terse parting note: "This isn't working. Let's make a clean break of it, shall we?"

Not knowing was the price she paid rushing into marriage like that. The most important relationship of her life, and she blew it. Young, impressionable, impatient, fearful of every rival glance, terrified of losing him.

A teen strolled in, saw her crying, and hurried on by avoiding eye contact. Paula sniffed and wiped her eyes and escaped into the corridor to hear herself being paged. Jake was waiting for her downstairs in the lobby.

"We're on our way to shop for an engagement ring. We thought we'd stop and see how things are going," he offered by way of explanation.

"Shelby's with you?"

Jake nodded. "She's upstairs, visiting a friend. How's it going with Joy and Colt?"

"I don't know. I couldn't stay." Humiliated by fresh tears, Paula fought them back. "I keep thinking how different things might have been if I'd just told Colt about Joy from the beginning."

"What's done is done," said Jake.

So why did she feel so undone? Unable to get quiet within, Paula led Jake outside to an open sunny space where she could relate the events of the morning without feeling like the walls were closing on her.

"Are you going?" asked Jake, upon learning of Walt Snyder's offer of safe haven.

"How can I? And Colt says he won't if I don't."

"You could go without him," he said.

"But it's Colt who's in real danger!"

"He's a survivor. He'll fend for himself."

That Jake's hard-nosed attitude bothered her was in itself bothersome. Paula dropped the subject, and went with Jake to the coffee shop where he had arranged to meet Shelby.

Shelby had arrived ahead of them, and was sitting with Walt Snyder. A petite young woman with red-gold curls, she was studious in repose. But she beamed to see them coming, tucked away her reading glasses and tipped her face for Jake's kiss.

Walt Snyder came to his feet as Paula introduced Jake.

"Monique's book caught my eye when I came in," explained Shelby as the men shook hands. "Mr. Snyder and Detective Browning were thumbing through it. I couldn't resist introducing myself as the editor."

"Where's Detective Browning?" asked Paula as she and Jake joined Shelby and Walt at the table.

"Checking with hospital security," Walt said. "He wanted them to know he's posting an officer outside Colt's door."

"Here's the postcard that's caused all the excitement," he added, and pointed out the card amid the collage of cards on the book cover. It was of Yellowstone Lodge. Both sides had been copied true to scale. The scenic side overlapped the message side just enough to obscure the postmarked date.

"You see why the card itself is so critical. Without a date, the card is meaningless," Walt explained.

Paula was distracted from the conversation

when she glanced up to see Joy angling toward their table. If her beaming face was any indication, her first meeting with Colt had gone well.

"Butter creams are Dad's favorite, too. He dozed off," offered Joy, her eyes as vivid as blue-eyed Marys blooming on creek banks. She turned to wing Jake an impudent grin. "You again. What are you doing here?"

"Shelby and I dropped by to see your mom a minute," said Jake.

Paula introduce Walt Snyder.

"How do you do, young lady?" Walt surveyed Joy with quick interest and pulled up a chair for her. They chatted briefly, then Walt turned back to Paula.

Unaware Paula knew of Detective Browning's offer to tuck them away until the danger passed, he spoke of it. "You will want to take Joy as well, just to be on the safe side."

"Colt told me," Paula said. "I appreciate your concern, Mr. Snyder. But I don't believe it's necessary."

Joy pressed prayerful hands together. "Please, Mom! It could be all the family vacations I've never had rolled into one."

"With school in session? I don't think so."
Concerned about work, and guilty that her sisters were currently doing their part for Gram as well as hers, she added, "Anyway, I miss Gram Kate. Don't you?"

"Oh, Mom. She doesn't even know us half the time," groused Joy.

Paula thinned her mouth in silent reprimand. Joy lowered her eyes, looking ashamed.

Walking that thin line between good parenting and grace, Paula offered, "How about some orange juice? They have a breakfast menu, too, if you're hungry."

Joy ordered a soft drink instead and drank it in silence. At length, she excused herself, saying she was going back up to see her father.

Relieved she had stopped sulking, Paula said, "I'll be up in a little while."

Joy's expression brightened. "Great. I'll tell him you're coming." She smiled at Mr. Snyder. "It was nice meeting you, Sir. See you later, Uncle Jake, Shelby. Make that *Aunt* Shelby."

Paula's heart lifted at Joy's acknowledgment of Jake and Shelby's engagement. It was equally satisfying to see Shelby flush with pleasure. Joy's departure broke up the gathering. Mr. Snyder relinquished Shelby's book with kind words for her editorial skills.

Paula walked Jake and Shelby to the main entrance. On her way back through the lobby, she was surprised to find Walt Snyder waiting for her.

"I don't mean to be a nuisance, but if I could have a word with you?" With a sweep of his hand, he ushered her to a nearby padded bench.

Mystified, Paula sat down.

"Colt is more than a talented writer, he's a good friend," said Walt, joining her on the bench. "I know about your estrangement, and appreciate how awkward that makes things. Suppose Detective Browning arranged for separate accommodations? Would you go then?"

Paula shot Walt an appraising glance. He appeared to be a careful man, not given to alarming people unnecessarily. Perhaps she should reconsider it. Vacillating, Paula asked for a little time to think about it.

"Certainly," he said, and reached for her hand. "Thank you, Paula. I'll be returning with Colt's laptop later today. We can talk then."

* * *

When he had gone, Paula made her way to the elevator. En route to Colt's floor, she tilted her head at the sound of a distant alarm. The ringing grew louder as the elevator doors opened.

A short, slender young man in a clerical collar and dark suit was waiting for the elevator. A hat rode low on his brow, shadowing his eyes and fine-boned face. He was carrying a Bible and wore a hospital pass that identified him as clergy.

Paula stopped on the elevator threshold, holding the door. "Is there a fire?"

"No, no. Just a false alarm," the young man replied in soothing tenor tones. "See there? They've turned off the racket."

"That's a relief!" Paula let go her caught breath. "Thank you, sir."

"Glad to be of some help. Peace, my friend." He lifted his hand.

Paula returned the gesture and hurried on her way. There was a cluster of nurses at a bend in the hallway. From a distance, it looked as if they were milling very near Colt's door. Apprehensions freshening, Paula quickened her pace, only to find Joy surrounded by nurses.

"Joy? Joy! What's wrong? What is it?" Paula bolted into their midst.

Joy burst into tears and flew into Paula's leaden arms. Braced for the worst, Paula gathered her tight. "Is it your dad? What's happened? Tell me, baby."

"You have to get out of here, it isn't safe." Joy buried a sob in Paula's neck and the rest of her explanation with it.

"What are you saying? Please, honey. Take a breath now, and tell me." Paula gripped Joy's shoulders and held her away, trying to read her face.

"This awful man!" wailed Joy, between sobs. "He asked me who I was and I told him and he said, 'Is your mother with you?' I remembered what Mr. Snyder said and thought he'd come to hurt you and Daddy, so I screamed. He hissed at me to hush, and when I didn't, he grabbed me by the shoulders and he…he said…"

Paula gripped Joy's arms, urging, "He said *what?* Go on, honey. Tell me!"

"'Stop that racket! Stop it, I say! It's a bad day to die!' Mom, I was so scared, I lost my voice! I couldn't even breathe until he let go and hurried away. I ran the other way. But I couldn't find a nurse. So I broke the glass on the fire alarm and then they all came!''

Inconsolable, Joy clung to Paula, shaking and sobbing pitifully.

''He had such weird eyes, Mom,'' wept Joy, fingers digging into Paula's arms. ''They were...like...haunted and desperate and...I don't know, just weird. You've got to get out of here. Somewhere safe.''

The hair on Paula's neck stood on end. But she comforted Joy, holding her, patting, offering soft murmurings. ''There, there. Mom's got you. No one's hurt. Everything will be fine.''

A nurse discreetly urged them into an office where they were joined by the head of hospital security, who introduced himself as George McDonnell. Joy collected her composure and repeated her story.

''I thought the police had posted a guard outside your husband's door,'' said Mr. McDonnell.

''So I was told,'' said Paula.

Mr. McDonnell promptly rose from his chair and went to look into it. Paula took Joy's hand

and caught up with the security man just as he let himself into Colt's unguarded room.

Colt was sleeping. Joy whispered his name, but he didn't stir. Turning away, she bumped the wheeled stand. A business card fluttered to the floor. The hospital security man stooped to retrieve it. He held it to the light.

"Reed Custer." His gaze shifted to Paula. "Do you know the name?"

"I don't think so," said Paula, too upset to be certain of anything. "But Colt may, if we can wake him."

A nurse who had followed them in reminded Paula that rest was critical to Colt's healing.

As they were talking, Detective Browning arrived accompanied by a red-faced uniformed officer. Due to a miscommunication, the officer had been guarding the wrong door. The hospital was searched. But the man who had so terrified Joy was gone without a trace.

Colt awakened at dusk, still in pain but more rested. The sense of quiet peace that had accompanied his deep sleep carried the moment as he realized Paula was in the room. He recognized her favorite scent, a light fragrance that reminded him of rain-washed lilies. Turning his head, he found her with her back to his window. Her brow was deeply furrowed, her demeanor fractured. Her makeup had faded. Her hair tumbled down her shoulders. Like a cloud fringed in sunlight, she was lovely even in her disarray.

"Where's Joy?" he asked.

"On the phone with her homeroom teacher, making arrangements. I've changed my mind. We're going into hiding." Paula's sky-blue eyes appraised him as she came to a rest at the side of his bed. "How are you feeling?"

"Better," said Colt.

Momentarily, her face showed relief. Then the cork came out of the bottle. Colt listened in growing alarm as she recounted in a harried rush all that had transpired while he slept.

"Joy's involved now. I can't take chances. Detective Browning's with her right now. He's going to see us safely to the airport. He also posted a man at your door," Paula said, seeking to quiet his alarm.

"You're leaving right away then?"

"Within the hour."

She had every right to condemn him. And yet, she retreated without reproach and returned to the window where the setting sun had turned the sky harvest gold. Colt imagined leaves rustling as she raked her hand through bright-hued hair.

Colt stirred the top sheet with his toes. "I'm sorry I got you into this mess. I could tell you not to fret, but…"

"I'm not fretting," claimed Paula. "Not about our physical safety, anyway. But I'm thinking of Joy. She wants a real family vacation. She said as much."

"The vacation or a 'real family?'" Colt replied.

"That's what concerns me."

Colt heard her draw a ragged breath and caught his own, waiting.

"The plan is for you to join us as soon as you're well enough," she said finally.

"Maybe they'll bring in Burwell and his thugs right away, and you can return home," Colt offered.

"I hope so," said Paula fervently. "But if not, and you join us, we need to be on our toes and guard Joy against any delusions about our getting back together."

Her warning evoked conflicting yearnings in

Colt. Guarding them, he asked, "How do you plan to do that?"

"For starters, we'll watch our words." Paula turned back to the bed. She entreated his understanding with a graceful gesture of an upturned hand. "I don't mean to nitpick. I mention it only because it's the kind of thing Joy could seize upon and use to support false hopes."

"Go on," he said, and braced himself.

"You called me 'babe' yesterday."

Colt frowned. It seemed so unlikely that he would let that long-ago pet name slip, he asked, "Was I fully conscious?"

Her skin pinked. "*Before* your accident. With those men," she added.

Colt remembered, then. He hadn't used her name because he hadn't wanted her assailant to know her by name. He apologized, and let it go, saying, "Is there anything else?"

"Just help me protect her. Emotionally, I mean. If we're polite with one another. Noncombative. But…well…"

"Distant?" he offered.

"Reserved." She picked her own way. "Nonpresumptuous. Considerate of one another's privacy.''

"Fair enough. Is that it?'' he asked.

"About Joy, yes.''

Anticipating, he said, "If it helps to rail on me, go ahead. I never should have involved you in this.''

"What's done is done.'' Paula paced to the window, and turned her back to the sunset glow. "There is just one more thing, Colt.''

"Oh?''

"You said you couldn't live with me then or now, and I guess I feel the same. But it has nothing to do with Mom and Dad's accident. I just wanted you to know that. Because if you blamed yourself then, or now…'' She faltered. Her voice quavered and fell to a somber funeral parlor hush. "I don't, and you shouldn't, either. That's all.''

Her words bore down on traumas too painful for the light of day. He dug his one good heel into the mattress and turned his face away. But he couldn't escape the flooding emotions, not with her presence filling the room. Her tender spirit. Her scent. Beguiling, but painful to his parched soul.

Colt held his breath as she fingered a decorative doodad adorning her pocketbook. His heart quickened as her gaze met his.

"I guess they told you Dr. Sandrelli has to release you from his care before you can follow," she said, filling the silence.

Colt nodded. He couldn't withstand a move just yet.

"I should go," she said, but didn't.

It hurt just to breath. Wanting the goodbying behind them, Colt stretched out his hand. "Godspeed."

Paula retraced her steps. Her hand met his. The palm he remembered from all those years ago had lost its soft plumpness. Her fingers were slim and firm and youthfully strong. Her nails were all natural, denuded of the bright polish for which she had once exhibited a fondness. Gone, too, was the lover's touch. It was a working hand now, and impersonal. A hand equal to the multiple tasks of business and home and mothering. He squeezed what he had forfeited the right to caress.

"Give Joy my love." Colt released her hand, and watched her go without a backward glance.

Was she sincere, saying she didn't blame him? The idea was too new, like a stone raked from the fire. Be it a common rock or a precious cornerstone, it was too hot to inspect.

Chapter Seven

Detective Browning's idea of "safe refuge" turned out to be a hidden-in-plain-view approach. He passed Paula her tickets just short of the congested security check at Chicago's international airport.

"Gatlinburg? Awesome!" chirped Joy.

"It's a nice vacation town, nestled in the heart of the Smoky Mountains. You'll be invisible among all those milling tourists. Relax and enjoy." The detective gave Paula a brochure depicting a comfortable lodge.

As it turned out, the brochure didn't do the place justice. The sprawling log-cabin lodge was eye-appealing and came with all the amenities, including a computer. The main body of their suite was comprised of a sunny living-dining area with a fully equipped galley kitchen. In addition to two bedrooms with a shared bathroom, there was an overflow alcove decorated in a garden theme, with a daybed covered in luscious florals. Two sets of double glass doors offered access to a terrace that wrapped their corner of the building. The terrace itself offered twin views, one of a mountain stream, while the other looked out on the swimming pool. Next door a smaller suite awaited Colt's arrival.

It was early September and unseasonably warm in the bustling mecca for tourists. There had been no occasion to pack for the trip, so Paula and Joy spent Tuesday shopping. Lack of sleep finally caught up with Paula. She slept soundly through the night and half the morning. Joy trotted in and opened her blinds to a flood of sunshine.

"Wake up, Mom. We got an e-mail from Dad. Dr. Sandrelli moved him to a private rehab center, but he won't release him to join us. Not until he can get around on crutches."

Paula had been dreaming she was in the hospital elevator. Since leaving Chicago, she had gone over that incident the way she might inspect a malfunctioning sign.

What was it about that minister that kept pestering her subconscious? Unable to pin it down, Paula slipped out of bed and into the satiny pink robe she had bought the previous day. "Did he say when that will be?"

"Friday or maybe Saturday," said Joy, visibly disappointed.

"We could be back home by then, if the police find Mr. Burwell and his hired thug. Any word on that?" asked Paula, sliding her feet into her pink slippers.

"No, nothing," said Joy. "But Dad promised he'd keep us informed."

Colt e-mailed them again when Hunter Cates posted bail. The police put a tail on him, hoping he would lead them to Burwell, his accomplice or both. But the days passed without any leads in the case. As for Monique, she went unmentioned in Colt's e-mails.

Curious as to whether that was an oversight or in some way significant, Paula bought a copy of Monique's book. She sunned herself beside the pool on Saturday, their fifth full day at the lodge, and perused Monique's book jacket. The picture on the back flap was that of a lovely young woman with deep set eyes, full lips and wildfire hair. Paula lay the book on the pavement beside her chaise longue, flipped over, tummy down, ankles crossed, and took off her sunglasses for a closer look at Monique's picture. She was squinting in the bright light when abruptly, shade fell over the book jacket.

Paula arched her back and turned on one elbow to find Colt resting on his crutches. He was tall and thin and shockingly haggard in his summer-weight pleated trousers, crisp shirt and dark tie. His left leg was encased in a padded brace, rather than the heavy plaster cast she had anticipated. The sun glinting off the adjacent swimming pool made reflecting pools of his eyes. In them was a catlike vigilance.

Checking the urge to fly for her inches-out-of-reach cover-up, Paula curled to a sitting position. "So they let you go."

"Finally," Colt said. "Where's Joy?"

"She's in her room studying. She's going to school online."

"Yes, I know."

"Any word on Burwell?" Paula changed the subject.

"No. Or the driver. And Cates is being a model citizen."

Paula couldn't get past his gauntness. Taking an indirect approach to his health, she asked, "Are you skipping rope yet?"

He smiled faintly at her borrowed expression. "No ropes. Just breakfast. Maybe we can grab a bite to eat when Joy finishes her studies?"

"We'll see," said Paula.

Expression placid, Colt ventured, "Mind if I join you?"

"Please do. Here, let me," Paula offered as he looked around for a chair.

"I can get it," Colt protested, though he wasn't entirely sure that was true.

"No need," she said, already en route.

Colt noted her slender carriage and a figure that did justice to her modest tropical-green one-piece swimsuit. Though *modest* he supposed, was a relative term. He hadn't seen that much of her since their tender days as newlyweds. It seemed a lifetime ago, a speck on the calendar. Now, to track those slim limbs and enchanting curves was to covet what no longer belonged to him.

Pivoting with the chair, Paula ran headlong into his silent appraisal. For a breath-caught moment, it was a standoff. If points were scored by not being the first to lower one's eyes, it ended in a tie.

"What do you call that shade of green?" Colt asked at length.

"My suit?" Paula considered the bright fabric through her sunglasses. "I'm not sure. Why? You wanna borrow my shades?"

Colt chuckled at her glibness. "Vivid, and very becoming."

Paula took the compliment with a grain of salt, and held out his chair. "Would you like it facing pool or the trees?"

"Here beside yours is fine," he said, and thanked her for her trouble.

"You're welcome."

Her expression was inscrutable, her eyes obscured by her dark glasses. But her pulse beat in the slim recess of her throat where moisture gathered like dewdrops and trickled down into that valley of forbidden attractions.

Colt's leg throbbed, though the pain couldn't

extinguish what the one glance had ignited. He pivoted on his good leg, maneuvered into the chaise longue and slid his crutches beneath it. He closed his eyes and waited for the waves of pain to stop.

"Are you doing okay?" Paula's tone gentled some.

"Miserable flight. We hit turbulence." Unwilling to admit how weak six days in the hospital had left him, Colt locked his hands behind his head and sighed in something close to contentment. "Sun feels good, doesn't it? The mountains are so lush, they even smell green. I could get used to this."

Paula slipped into her swimsuit cover-up while his eyes were closed. "How's your article for *Profile Magazine* coming?"

"On hold, until the missing pieces—or I should say people—fall into place." Colt's lids fluttered open. He indicated Monique's book on the foot of the chaise longue. "I see you're reading *Wish You Were Here*. What do you make of it?"

"Okay, I guess. If you like that sort of thing."

"She was able to move out of the mission

and get herself a place with the advance.'' Colt shot Paula an intuitive glance. ''You haven't read this, have you?''

''All right, so I haven't. Though I *did* read the book jacket.'' Indicating Monique's picture with a pink-tipped toe, Paula added, ''I can't see much of a resemblance, by the way.''

''To you?'' he said.

''Except for the hair.'' Paula lifted her hair and piled it atop her head. She held it there, enjoying the breeze on her neck. ''What's the status with Monique? Have you heard from her?''

''No, not yet. It could be that she's avoiding me,'' he admitted.

''Oh?'' ventured Paula, more curious than she cared to be. ''Why's that?''

''I think she set me up at her house when Burwell's pals came calling.''

''You mean she was expecting trouble and didn't tell you?'' Processing the information, Paula let her hair drift back to her shoulders. ''That wasn't very friendly.''

''No. But it *would* explain why she's not answering my e-mails.''

Paula made a face. "What do you see in this woman, anyway?"

"She's an enigma," replied Colt. "Who could predict an attractive, multitalented woman would hit rock bottom the way she did?"

"Why did she? Hit bottom, I mean."

"One bad decision—she fell in love with the wrong guy."

Skeptical, Paula replied, "If that's all there were to it, there'd be homeless shelters on every block."

Colt cocked her a gray-eyed glance. "When'd *you* get so cynical?"

"I'm not cynical. I'm just not convinced your friend's ex-husband is the root of all her problems," reasoned Paula.

"Bad husbands *make* bad marriages and I can't think of anything quite so bad as marrying a woman for her money, bleeding her dry, then taking her through a final cleaning in divorce court," said Colt. "Except murder. And by the look of it, Burwell could be guilty of that, too."

Privately, Paula had to agree that the guy sounded thoroughly despicable. "Whose idea was it to feature him in *Profile Magazine?*"

"Walt's. It galled him to see Burwell strutting around with his reputation intact and his business flourishing while his ex-wife was in a homeless shelter fending off a nervous breakdown.

"So I phoned Monique at the shelter about six months ago, introduced myself and told her I was interested in writing a piece on Simon Burwell. But she was down-and-out and didn't want to be interviewed. Walt gave it a little time, then suggested I approach her again. Which I did. Only this time, I passed myself off as homeless.

"Monique was feeling better," Colt continued. "She had overcome her depression and was working on a book. She gave me the lowdown on Burwell and said that she had a postcard that would turn the tables on him. Looking back, I suspect she wanted him to know as much and to buy her silence. Or at least make a bid."

Startled, Paula said, "You mean to say she was *blackmailing* him?"

"Or planned to, in hopes of recouping some of her financial losses. It would explain why she didn't go to the police with her postcard,'' reasoned Colt.

''I can understand her wanting what was rightfully hers. But to write a book just to prove she had the goods on the guy? That's crazy!'' Paula scratched her head. ''Why not just send him a photocopy of the postcard and name her price?''

''It would have been a lot simpler,'' agreed Colt. ''But Monique's full of quirky left-handed turns. That's what makes her story so fascinating.''

''You think?'' Paula sniffed. ''In her shoes I would have bid the louse good riddance, thanked God I'd survived the bad experience and moved ahead.''

''You would, and you have the record to prove it,'' agreed Colt.

Paula folded her sunglasses. ''I thought we were talking about Monique.''

''We were. But you distracted me with your philosophy on disrupted marriages.''

Peeved, she replied, ''Don't be so hard on yourself.''

''Maybe you've been hard enough for both of us,'' he countered evenly.

"Need I remind you who walked out on whom?" Paula shot back.

"So while you were thanking God, did you ever think maybe the honest thing to do would be to pick up the phone and tell me you were expecting my child?"

"That's rich, coming from the guy who passed himself off as homeless, stole a postcard and fled the scene all for a story. You're right, you know. Bad husbands *do* make bad marriages."

"Okay, okay," he conceded. "Make that 'the wise thing to do.' In fact, scratch it all together. I'm sorry. I didn't mean to bring up personal grievances. It's water under the bridge. Let's just be nice and I'll get back on track. How about it?"

"Very well, then." Paula curbed the impulse to toss his crutches in the pool and storm inside. "Finish your story."

"The *Tribune* called Monique about doing a review a couple of days before the sky fell in on her again." Colt picked up where he had left off. "She was euphoric, and in that state, offered to let me stay at her place while she was out of town."

"Lucky you."

"It was my opportunity to search for the postcard she'd mentioned," Colt continued as if uninterrupted. "She let me in on her way out and I was still searching when you arrived."

"Did she say where she was going?"

"Yes. Fox Creek Christian Retreat. She said her friend Patrick was paying her way."

Paula shot him an incredulous look. "Give me a break! This woman, this would-be blackmailer, trots off to a Christian retreat in the midst of her big moment—the release of her book and a splashy review in the *Trib?*"

"It was easy enough to check—Walt's church sponsored the retreat at Fox Creek," said Colt. "Though hindsight suggests Monique's hasty retreat was a convenient way to be out of Burwell's reach the day the review hit the paper."

"She might have warned you! It's no thanks to her that you weren't killed," said Paula, fanning herself with Monique's book jacket.

"Burwell had no ax to grind with me," reasoned Colt. "I doubt it occurred to Monique that I could become a casualty."

"Maybe. Or maybe she'd discovered you'd

deceived her, and figured let the chips fall where they may. She called Jake on Saturday night, and questioned him about you.''

''What'd Jake tell her?''

''He didn't tell her that you were a writer, if that's what you're getting at. He didn't know himself.''

''Easy, I'm not looking for another argument,'' said Colt. ''Just assembling the pieces, hoping to get a line on Monique and wrap up my story.''

''Is that all you can think about? Your story?'' Paula tossed the book jacket to one side and got to her feet. ''Monique involved innocent people in this mess. In case you don't know it, it was her number on Jake's caller ID that gave Joy a contact. It was the green light she needed to strike out in search of you.''

''Yes, but I returned Joy's call the moment I learned she was in the city and made sure she didn't come to Monique's house. She was out of harm's way when I went to work,'' Colt said hastily.

''You don't know Joy! Once she latches on to an idea, she's on the attack,'' countered Paula, hands on her hips. ''Nothing deters her.''

"Tenacity has its place."

"She ran away from home, Colt! I won't even let her ride her bike to the country, and here she was, on a bus to Chicago with no one to meet her. I shudder to think what *could* have happened."

Colt's gaze slid away as she went on to enumerate the possibilities. His sudden silence left her voice hanging out there like shredded chards. Heat flooded her cheeks.

Seeming at a loss for words, he loosened his tie. "Hot, isn't it?"

"It isn't the heat, it's the—" she began, then caught herself.

"Humidity," Colt finished.

He looked at her and she looked at him, lips parted, breath caught, remembering together that long-ago evening in her parents' Liberty Flats living room when he had arrived to pick her up for their first date. Except they were older now. Wiser. And this time she had every reason to be angry with him. No chance of grins and giggles building to shouts of laughter as they had that day over the shared realization they had skipped introductions that morning on the porch. He had asked her for a date and arrived to collect her, still not knowing her name.

"Why didn't you just ask me?" she had teased him about it later. In their brief marriage, the heat-humidity phrase had become a byword to drop whatever they had disagreed upon as if it had never existed, and make up. Shared memories hung between them, bittersweet, like winter fruit left to wither on the slumbering branch.

He began, "Remember when—"

"No, and you shouldn't be either." Paula tied her swimsuit cover-up with fumbling fingers. "I'll tell Joy you're here."

"You forgot your shoes," Colt called and shifted onto his crutches as she retraced her steps.

She grabbed her book and her cold drink, then arched her foot, reaching for a sandal. Colt caught one, then the other with a crutch, pushed them into position for her and spoke her name. Fingers in her hair, she lifted her face and with wary eyes, met his gaze.

"I've proved I don't know anything about being a parent." Colt downed fragmented pride and with it resentment over all her silence had cost him. "I *do* want to learn. I won't make the same mistake twice."

Tears brimmed in her eyes. Surprising to him, shaming to her. Rapidly blinking them away, she regained her composure. "You're welcome. Now if you'll excuse me, I need an aspirin."

Colt watched her retreat. He needed more than aspirin. His head was fine, but his soul was parched.

You're welcome, she'd said, as if it were no more than a casual courtesy. *Like fetching a chair.*

He sat down again. Hands locked behind his head, eyes closed, Colt recalled the day he threw down the car keys, emptied his wallet of all his cash and left it there on the kitchen table for Paula. He still remembered each word of the note he'd written all those years ago: "This isn't working. Let's make a clean break of it, shall we?"

He was deliberately austere in the writing. He hadn't said he was sorry. Her parents were dead. *Sorry* didn't cover a thing like that. He had nothing to give her except a chance to heal without living under the same roof with the cause of her pain. And he couldn't give her that if she perceived him as a sympathetic character in need of her forgiveness.

In those days, Paula's only flaw that he could see was being impressed with him as a rising star in the advertising world. He told her one evening as they prolonged the good-nighting on the porch of her parents' home, that serving as poster boy for the great outdoors wasn't that big of a deal.

Taken aback, she'd cried, "You're just being modest!"

It was hardly modest to protest that being embraced as a public heartthrob was a royal pain. So he didn't. Instead, he yielded to the impatient passion of youth and rushed Paula down the garden path in a quickly planned backyard wedding. His parents were out of the country on a mission trip and couldn't make the wedding. His sister was in the last week of a high-risk pregnancy and couldn't come, either. Nor could C.J., who was finishing a tour of duty in the military.

Sorry for Colt that his family wasn't part of the celebration, Paula radiated sensitivity at every turn. Past attractions paled by comparison. Life with Paula began so rich and full.

They had been married a month when they made their first trip back to Liberty Flats. Once there, Paula decided to stay a couple of days and have a real visit. Colt had just begun the drive home alone and was missing her already when he collided with her parents' vehicle on that rainy road.

What followed was a bleak and downhill blur as he and Paula lived and moved in isolated cells of pain. He walked on catpaws so as not to set off her hair-trigger tears, until it all imploded beneath his self-blame and he walked away, fearing she would come to loathe him.

Had she? Or was she, in the long view, thankful he had made the decision for them both, and spared her the guilt?

Colt had tried for years to come to terms with his own self-condemnation. But just when he thought he had outdistanced it, there it was, waiting. Weary of trudging the treadmill of his past, Colt struggled onto his crutches and went inside.

Chapter Eight

Colt had opened a torrential flood of memories Paula had long since relegated to the back files of her mind. Equally unsettling was the realization that Colt had grievances against *her* for not telling him she was expecting his child. Had she looked at it from his point of view, she might have expected as much. But she hadn't considered his vantage point.

Until now, when he got under her skin. She spoke her mind and he spoke his. Honesty was supposed to be the key to good communication. So why did she come away feeling like a shrew? Emotions fractured, Paula knocked on

Joy's open door to find her at her computer, still in her pajamas.

"Get dressed, Joy. You have company," said Paula.

The mouse went still in Joy's hand. She tipped her face, her heart in her eyes. "Daddy?" she asked on a caught breath.

At Paula's nod, Joy leaped to her feet. "Can I see him right now?"

"He's expecting you," said Paula.

Joy squealed and thrust her arm in the air. "Sweet! Are you coming, too, Mom?"

"We've already talked."

"Still, it would be polite if we, you know, went out of our way to make him feel welcome," pressed Joy.

"That's nice. He'll appreciate your efforts, I'm sure." Paula kept her voice neutral.

"Oh, boy. What to wear, what to wear?" Joy rattled through a shopping bag from a Gatlinburg boutique. "Maybe the skirt and blouse I bought yesterday. No, I wore a dress at the hospital, I don't want him thinking I'm prissy. I know! My new jeans and that funky lime T-shirt."

Battling conflicting emotions, Paula retreated

to her room. She changed out of her swimsuit and donned a silky tropical print skirt and shell that complimented her late-season tan. The long-sleeved overblouse that completed the ensemble was sheer, and perfect for a warm autumn day.

Hearing Joy still in her room, Paula knocked on her open door. "I thought you'd gone."

"I made Dad a get well-welcome card. This printer's really pokey," complained Joy.

"I'm going shopping for quilting supplies," said Paula. "Can I bring you anything?"

"No. I'm on my way." Joy snatched up her card from the printer, then turned before Paula. "How do I look?"

"Joyful." Holding back inexplicable tears, Paula hugged her. "Do you have any idea how precious you are?"

"Don't get sappy on me, Mom. I'm in a hurry." Flushed with eagerness, Joy squirmed free and made a beeline for the door that connected their suite to Colt's.

"Not that way." Paula stopped her. "Use the corridor entrance."

Joy rolled her eyes, and complied. But at the door, she turned back. "Come with me. Please?" she coaxed, until Paula capitulated.

Colt answered the bell. His scarred demeanor melted at the sight of Joy.

"I ordered a pizza. There's plenty, if you want to join us." He included Paula in the invitation.

"Thanks, maybe another time. I'm on my way out."

Paula blew Joy a kiss and a short while later sat down for a solitary lunch at a sidewalk café. The grilled chicken salad sandwich was delicious, but it didn't settle well. Face it, *she* was unsettled, part and parcel, and had been from the moment she glanced up to see it was Colt's shadow throwing shade where there had been sunlight.

God, my helper. Paula conveyed in snatches of prayer just how confused she was that she should feel any regard for Colt. This forced retreat was untimely and inconvenient. And not just to her. For Jake and her sisters and Gram Kate, too.

No scripture fell to mind. No ministering lyrics. No wordless impression. Restless within, Paula left the restaurant and ambled through the shopping district until she found a quilt shop where she purchased the items she needed to finish a quilt she had begun for Joy years earlier. At her request, Jake had sent it by mail. If she was ever going to finish the thing, now was the time.

It was midafternoon when she retired to the babbling creek side of the wraparound terrace. Joy and Colt were by the pool. She couldn't see them from where she was lounging, but the breeze carried their voices. Their words were indistinct. The overall tone was pleasant and punctuated with occasional laughter.

Paula settled in a chaise longue and closed her eyes. Without volition, the minister from the hospital elevator fell to mind. Something about that whole incident nagged at her. Was it relevant somehow to their present circumstances? Or safe to dismiss? Wishing she knew, Paula went inside and returned with her Bible. It fell open to I Corinthians 13. Seeking a respite for her spirit, she let her gaze walk down the page: ''Love is patient. Love is kind. It does not envy, it does not boast, it is not proud. It is not rude. It is not self-seeking, it is not easily angered, it keeps no record of wrongs.''

God's love. *The kind you're to model.* It kept

no record of wrongs. Paula looked away from the page as if bruised by the wounds of a friend.

Below, the creek trickled past like a wind-blown strand and lulled her to sleep. Slowly, her Bible slid off her lap. Paula awoke from sleep and faced the hurtful truth that she was indeed keeping a running account of Colt's wrongs against her.

"I don't want to be unforgiving, Lord. But I can't seem to shed this resentment. Here, you take it." Like a child throwing autumn leaves in the air, Paula lifted her hands in surrender. Bit by bit, her agitation quieted. The very air seemed scented with God's grace and kindness toward her.

But her peace was soon challenged by Joy, who sought her out with an invitation from Colt to join them for dinner.

"Thanks, but no," said Paula.

"So what are you going to do, hide out until we go home?" groused Joy.

"I'm going to work on your quilt. You go on and have a good time," replied Paula with pained affection.

Joy turned away, huffing. Following her with her gaze, Paula shrugged the knots from her shoulders. ''Keep tomorrow morning open for church.''

''Where?'' asked Joy shortly.

''Down the street. The one with the Biblical garden.'' Summer and autumn mixed in the colorful hues and varied shades of green that had caught Paula's eye as they had passed the church a few days ago. ''If the flock is receiving as much care as that lovely garden, we'll feel welcome, I'm sure.''

''Whatever.'' Visibly annoyed by Paula's refusal to have dinner with them, Joy went indoors to shower and change.

Paula followed at her leisure, put the quilt in her new lap frame and ate a salad and sandwich before going to work.

Joy returned home around nine o'clock that evening in a sunnier mood. She draped herself in a chair to sing Colt's praises and watch Paula quilt. Eventually, Paula's eyes blurred from the strain of close needlework. She put the quilt aside, kissed Joy and called it a night.

The next morning, Paula bathed in scented bubbles and dressed in pale pink. Form-fitting through the bust, waist and hips, the dress flared and wafted almost to her ankles, light as a summer breeze. She brushed a thread from the cap sleeve and spritzed her throat with her favorite scent. The hat that had been in her car the day the thugs tried to kidnap her was on a hook in the foyer.

Paula collected it and was on her way to the mirror when Joy plopped down on the sofa with an open box of cold cereal. Alert to her evaluating glance, Paula asked, "Something wrong?"

"You missed a button." Joy pointed it out.

Paula looked down the row of pearl buttons closing the bodice of her dress. They extended several inches below the dropped waist. Her freshly lacquered nails tapped the last pearl as she fit it to the embossed hole on her way to the mirror where she straightened her hat. Meeting Joy's reflection in the glass, she turned and braced herself. "What now?"

"Nothing. You look nice. I was just thinking—you and Daddy must have been a knock-out couple."

Paula bit back the cautionary words. "That's sweet," she said instead. "Now where are my car keys? Finish your breakfast, and let's scoot."

Love Inspired®

"When I found these Love Inspired novels, I found hope."

– BEVERLY D., BUFFALO, NY

LETTERS FROM READERS
WHOSE HEARTS WERE
TOUCHED BY OUR
UNIQUE BRAND OF
INSPIRATIONAL ROMANCE.

Now it's your turn to fall in love with

Love Inspired ®

> "We all need a little romance in our lives and this wholesome, inspirational series is exactly what I have been looking for."
> – Karen K., Warner, AB

> "It's a pleasure to read good, interesting, clean in thought, word and character books."
> – Bonnie L., Basile, LA

> "I love this series. It lifts my spirits."
> – Laura R., Nanuet, NY

> "Thank you...I will not be ashamed to share these with my granddaughter who has become interested in reading since she always sees me with a book close by."
> – M.L., Joshua Tree, CA

Scratch the silver area, complete and return the card on the right to receive your 2 FREE *Love Inspired*® books.

These books have a combined cover price of $9.00 in the U.S. and $10.50 in Canada, but they are yours free!

Visit us online at
www.LoveInspiredBooks.com

Each of your *FREE* Love Inspired titles is filled
with joy, faith and family values.

Books received may
not be as shown.

Scratch off the silver area
to see what the Steeple
Hill Reader Service has
waiting for you!

YES! Please send me the **2 FREE** Love Inspired® books
and **FREE GIFT** for which I qualify. I understand that I am under
no obligation to purchase any books as explained on the back
of this card.

313 IDL DVG2   113 IDL DVGZ

FIRST NAME   LAST NAME

ADDRESS

APT.#   CITY

STATE/PROV.   ZIP/POSTAL CODE   (LI-TE-04)

Steeple Hill Reader Service™—Here's How It Works:

If offer card is missing write to: Steeple Hill Reader Service, 3010 Walden Ave., P.O. Box 1867, Buffalo NY 14240-1867

BUSINESS REPLY MAIL
FIRST-CLASS MAIL   PERMIT NO. 717-003   BUFFALO, NY

POSTAGE WILL BE PAID BY ADDRESSEE

STEEPLE HILL READER SERVICE
3010 WALDEN AVE
PO BOX 1867
BUFFALO NY 14240-9952

NO POSTAGE
NECESSARY
IF MAILED
IN THE
UNITED STATES

* * *

Home health care service provided Colt with a nurse to give both professional care and practical help at the beginning and end of each day. In her late fifties, Joan Hilbert arrived at daybreak, per Colt's request. She pressed his suit and chatted amicably about her husband, children and grandchildren while he shaved, then facilitated his bathing and dressing. Colt turned down her offer to cook his breakfast, and asked her for a lift to the church instead.

The back pew extended out farther than the rest. The open space in front of it accommodated Colt's injured leg. As a youth he had attended worship faithfully. But after his split with Paula, Colt found little solace in the midst of those enjoying a peace that eluded him. His work at the magazine became a welcome distraction from the wintry landscape within. So he gave it his full attention, including weekends. Now, after years of neglect, being in Sunday morning worship was about as comfortable as scrubbing his teeth with someone else's toothbrush.

But Joy had invited him and he couldn't

bring himself to disappoint her. Hearing voices, Colt turned to see Joy crossing the church vestibule. His paternal glow overlapped his conflicting emotions concerning Paula who trekked after her, a cloud in pink. Colt straightened his tie, spread one arm over the back of the pew and beckoned to them. Joy's face lit up.

"Look, Mom. Dad's here!"

Colt read Joy's lips as she pointed him out to Paula. Clearly she hadn't been expecting him. She ducked her head, taking cover beneath a wide-brimmed hat. Embellished with netting and an old-fashioned cabbage rose, the hat was familiar and fetching. Her hair curled beneath the brim, and spilled to her shoulders in rich radiant waves.

Joy's bejeweled fingers fluttered hello as she entered the pew from the other end, and plunked down beside him.

"Hi, Dad!"

"Hi, yourself," he answered her bid for a smile, and braced himself for Paula.

"Oops. Forgot something." Joy popped up again.

Paula bit back a protest, pulled in high-heeled sandals that left her toes exposed and let

Joy pass. Her nails were tipped in glossy pink enamel. The same feminine hue adorned her fingertips.

"Good morning. I hope I'm not intruding," ventured Colt. "Joy invited me."

"I guessed as much," said Paula. "How are you feeling?"

"Better."

"Then Joy didn't wear you out last night?"

"No, not at all."

"Don't let her push you beyond your limits. Just tell her when you need to rest."

Finding her sudden consideration as suspect as it was surprising, Colt was relieved when her gaze shifted away from him to the cross upon the dais. Her lashes came down, then swept apart as she looked past those stark wooden beams to a stained-glass window depicting the Shepherd with a lamb in his arms.

Their own intrepid lamb returned waving a bulletin. She nudged Paula to the middle, and continued to crowd her closer to Colt as more people filed in. Colt and Paula soon sat shoulder to shoulder. Paula fanned herself with an old-fashioned pasteboard fan garnered from the hymnal rack, imbuing the air with her light fragrance.

The song leader stepped up and bid them rise and sing. Gamely, Colt rose on his crutches. Paula shared her hymnal and sang with a sweet abandon that contrasted the depleted places in Colt.

At the worship leader's request, they joined hands for prayer. Having kept his distance all these years, approaching God in prayer seemed the height of hypocrisy. Yet as Colt battled not to pray, the fragrance of his Heavenly Father's mercy tantalized him as never before. His limbs ached, his palms were damp by the time the prayer ended, and Paula withdrew her hand.

A frail white-haired gentleman stepped up to the pulpit, opened his Bible and launched a well-crafted sermon aimed at exposing the father of lies, the hidden face behind every deception dating back to the Garden of Eden.

He spoke of the patriarch Jacob deceiving his blind father into giving him his elder twin's inheritance. He cited David's deceit in sending Bathsheba's husband Uriah to certain death on the battlefield. Digging deep into the Scriptures, he exposed the darker side of Biblical hero after hero.

Just when it seemed none would escape the pervasive and sly deceit of the enemy, the pastor reminded his flock of God's mercy and grace through Christ Jesus.

"Marvel upon wonders, God doesn't just forgive, he forgets the trespass," the aged pastor concluded, and read in closing verses from the 103rd Psalm:

"The Lord is compassionate and gracious, slow to anger, abounding in love. He will not always accuse, nor will He harbor His anger forever; He does not treat us as our sins deserve, or repay us according to our iniquities. For as high as the heavens are above the earth, so great is His love for those who fear Him; as far as the east is from the west, so far has He removed our transgressions from us. As a father has compassion on his children, so the Lord has compassion on those who fear Him for he knows how we are formed. He remembers that we are dust."

The air had grown stuffy, the room too close for comfort. Forgiveness, attractive though it

was, couldn't bring back Paula's parents. Or re-
store Colt's fractured marriage. Or return the
wide slice of Joy's childhood, forever lost to
him. Resolute, Colt got his crutches beneath
him. When the benediction came, he moved
into the aisle and out the door.

"Wait for me, Dad. I'm coming," said Joy,
following at his heels.

Chapter Nine

Paula exited the church, thinking once more of the minister who had reassured her over the false fire alarm. She returned the incident to the mental hook from which it kept falling, and looked across the churchyard to see Colt perched on a low stone wall with his crutches beside him.

He lifted his head at her approach. His scarred demeanor was impossible to read. Not so with Joy. Her lilting voice and sparkling laughter carried on the light breeze.

"What's so funny?" Paula asked.

"Dad. His tummy's rumbling like a volcano.'' Joy linked arms with Colt. ''He thinks he can walk back to the lodge....''

''Walking's part of my therapy. Doctor's orders. It's only a block and a half,'' said Colt.

''...but I told him you'd give him a ride. You will, won't you?'' Joy talked right over him.

''Sure, no problem.'' Sensitive to Colt's reserve, Paula took the initiative and asked, ''Would you like to stop for lunch first?''

''Food, food! Please, Dad? I'm starving,'' cried Joy.

''I guess we had better feed you, then,'' Colt yielded.

The Great Smoky Mountains National Park had been so designated by Roosevelt in 1940. The verdant, awe-inspiring beauty of the place was evident throughout Gatlinburg, nestled as it was amidst forested mountain slopes. The locals, no less tenacious and enduring than the craggy boulders strewn along creek beds and campsites and forest trails, capitalized on their down-home heritage. ''Hillbilly'' was their bread and butter. They spelled it out in neon on everything from hotels to hoedown halls to mom-and-pop restaurants.

Paula parked the car at one such country affair set in the heart of the strip. Mismatched tables painted in a bold checkerboard pattern were scattered over the scuffed wooden floor. The hostess seated them at the wide front window. Stiffly starched curtains framed a view of the street. Crowded and comfortable, the place exuded a rustic charm that was as relaxed and informal as the freckled waitress who took their order. She soon returned with enough food for a family twice their size.

"How're we doing, folks? Need anything?"

"Just coffee, thanks." Colt nudged his empty cup into position at the edge of the table.

The waitress poured Paula a fresh cup, too, and gave Colt the check. The apron from which she withdrew it was decorated with a child's handprints, done in finger paints.

Joy indicated her apron. "Look, Mom! Hand prints."

"I see." Smiling, Paula asked the waitress about her apron and learned that her children had made it for her.

"A treasure, isn't it?"

Paula chimed agreement. The waitress hurried away. Joy told Colt, "Mom's quilting me a treasure, too."

Surprise flickered in Colt's gray gaze. "I didn't know you sewed," he said to Paula.

"I learned in 4-H. But it was Mom and Gram Kate who taught me to quilt," said Paula. "Say grace for us, would you, Joy?"

Joy did so. But over breakfast she returned to the subject of the quilt and with minimal input from Paula, explained how at her first birthday party family and friends had dipped their hands in fabric paint and left their prints on individual quilt blocks.

"We're calling it *Helping Hands.*"

"Good choice," said Colt. "I wish I'd been on board to help."

"It's not too late," piped Joy. "Mom can teach you to quilt. Can't you, Mom?"

Seeing through Joy's thinly veiled attempt to throw them together, Paula raised her coffee cup with a noncommittal, "Finish your breakfast, Joy."

"I can't. I'm stuffed." Pushing her chair back, Joy patted her tummy, then cocked her head. "Hear that? The jukebox has stopped yodeling. Who has change?"

Colt retrieved a handful of coins from his pocket. Joy thanked him and sped off to the jukebox. Watching their buffer go, Paula felt the sudden silence eating away at her hard-won ease.

Colt was looking after Joy, too. "She was cute about the quilt. Is she helping you with it?"

"Are you kidding? She can't sit still long enough to thread a needle."

"She'll outgrow the wiggles one of these days, don't you think?"

"But will I live to see it?" quipped Paula.

Colt chuckled, and went on to confide his own interest in quilts, an interest that had begun when he had reviewed a book about quilts and the underground railroad.

"It's been a couple of years, but the book is still fresh in my mind," he said.

"What was the title again?"

"Hidden in Plain View," replied Colt.

At his response, the very thing that had been eluding Paula for days fell into place. She gave a shout. "That's it! He was hidden in plain view! The same idea Detective Browning had for us here in Gatlinburg. How could I miss it?"

Colt blinked at her outburst. "I beg your pardon?"

"The minister coming off the elevator!" cried Paula. "He blended right in!"

Colt scratched his head. "You *have* lost me now. What minister? What elevator?"

"At the hospital last week!"

Joy returned before Paula could explain further. She divided an anxious glance between the two of them. "I heard Mom clear across the room. You aren't arguing, are you?"

"No. Just talking," said Paula quickly. "Aren't you going to play a song?"

"I can't find any I know," claimed Joy.

Colt pushed back his plate and pulled out his wallet. "Then go pay the tab for us, would you please?"

Joy held out her hand for the money, then trotted away on her errand.

"Now, then. About this minister?" Colt prompted Paula when they were alone.

Paula strained forward, confiding, "Maybe I'm obsessing. But my subconscious keeps offering up this pastor guy, as if I've missed something. Know what I mean?"

"Sure. Happens enough, you learn to listen,"

said Colt, nodding. He sat forward as well, narrowing the distance between them. Hands locked together on the table just inches from her laced fingers, he suggested, "Let's go over it together. Start at the beginning."

Encouraged, Paula related to the best of her memory her encounter with the man in the hospital elevator. "His Bible and clerical dress, even his parting 'Peace' was what you'd expect from a minister," she said, winding to a close. "But the timing was such that I'm now asking myself what if he was just pretending to be a minister? What if he was…"

"The guy who accosted Joy?" Colt anticipated her suspicions.

"Exactly!"

"How about her description? Did it fit the guy you saw?"

"What there was of it, yes. But Joy was badly frightened. Her description was broad, you could shape it to fit almost anyone," admitted Paula.

"The man you saw, was he wearing a name tag?"

"He had on a pass that signified he was clergy. As for a name…" Paula paused. She drummed the table with her fingertips, then opened one hand, gesturing her uncertainty. "If so, the name didn't register with me. Why? What have you got there?" Paula asked, as Colt withdrew a card from his wallet.

"Walt's pastor's calling card. He came to see me at the hospital the same day Joy was there. I was asleep. But he left this."

Paula's fingers brushed Colt's as the card changed hands. "Pastor Reed Custer." She read the name. "I remember now. Joy brushed against your table, and a card fell to the floor. Is this the same one?"

"Must be," said Colt.

Paula processed this new information. Frowning, she voiced her growing confusion. "So was elevator man a thug in disguise? Or a minister making hospital calls? Will we ever know?"

"Maybe, by process of elimination."

"My goodness! You're right. Has anyone talked to Pastor Custer?"

"Not that I know of," said Colt.

"We should call him, then. He could have seen something in the corridor that no one else saw. If he was at the right place at the right time, anyway,'' added Paula.

"Exactly,'' said Colt.

"But let's not say anything to Joy unless it becomes relevant,'' cautioned Paula. Seeing Joy coming their way, she lowered her voice and explained, "She's subject to nightmares, and I'd rather not rehash it unnecessarily.''

"I'll call Walt's pastor as soon as we return to the lodge,'' agreed Colt.

Chapter Ten

Paula was alone in their main living area slipping out of her shoes when Colt knocked. She noted with a sweeping glance dark shadows underscoring his eyes.

"Come in." Paula eased the way by holding the door with her stockinged foot. She gestured toward the sofa. "Did you reach Pastor Custer?"

"Not yet. There won't be anyone in the church office until tomorrow morning. But I left my number and a message to call me."

"Make yourself comfortable while I check on Joy. I think she's changing her clothes."

Paula was nearing Joy's door when it flew

open. She popped out and angled Colt a happy grin. "I thought I heard voices. Did Mom show you the quilt?"

"Not yet. I'll get it," said Paula. But before changing direction, she warned Joy in a whisper, "He looks tired. He might rather do this another time."

"You think?" Joy scratched her head, then trotted to Colt's side. "Mom's worried you're not up for this. You could stretch out right here on our sofa, and take a nap if you want to, Dad. We've got all afternoon to look at the quilt."

Paula crimped her mouth at Joy's transparent ploy. She gathered the quilt off the foot of her bed and hurried back before the little match-maker took further advantage.

Joy met her dark glance with an innocent, "I was just telling Dad we could do this later."

"Yes, I heard," interrupted Paula. Attention shifting to Colt, she added, "But as long as you're here…"

"See?" said Joy, pointing as Paula held up the quilt for Colt's review. "A handprint from everyone in the family and some friends, too."

Colt whistled appreciatively. "That is nice."

Pleased, Joy snatched the quilt away and

spread it over Colt's lap. Colt touched a tiny handprint. "Is this yours?"

"Yep. J-O-Y, see?"

Paula retreated to a nearby armchair as Joy showed off the identifying names embroidered beneath each hand. It was a lengthy acquainting that followed. But in so doing, Joy brought Colt up to speed on her family, hand by hand.

Colt fingered the neatly melded strips bordering the blocks.

"This piece here is cut from my homecoming gown," offered Joy.

"Since when do junior highers go to homecoming?" asked Colt.

Joy giggled. "I meant as a newborn. The gown I wore home from the hospital. See this white satin scrap? It's from the angel costume I wore one year in the Christmas pageant."

"Good casting," said Colt.

Joy wrinkled her nose. "Uncle Jake didn't think so. He said I was a wild child with my hair standing out in every direction."

"It had nothing to do with your curls," Paula spoke up. "It was your antics on stage."

"I was little. So what if I picked the poinsettias?"

"And scattered the petals," said Paula.

Colt's hand crept to his shirtfront, bracing his chest wound as he laughed. Nor could Paula hold back a smile. Feeling better for it, she filled in the blanks as Joy traced the assortment of fabrics that bordered the quilt blocks.

"The gingham print is from Gram Kate's favorite apron. This pink is from a nightgown the girls and I bought for Mom's birthday one year," she said, pointing. "The white here was snipped from Dad's Sunday shirt. See this plaid flannel scrap? It came from Jake's favorite work shirt."

Glancing up, Paula found Colt's gaze had shifted from the quilt to her. "Are you bored yet?" she asked, cheeks heating.

"Not a bit," he claimed. "I like knowing the roots of things. Carry on."

"That's about it. Just a few snippets from Joy's outgrown baby dresses. That and some hand-me-downs from my sisters and assorted family members." Paula brought her summary to a close.

"If this quilt is any indication, I'd say love has you covered, Joy," said Colt.

"I sure do wish there was something of you in it, too, Dad," replied Joy.

"Then thread me a needle and I'll help quilt it." Colt looked to Paula for permission. "Is that okay with you?"

"Certainly." Covering her surprise, Paula retrieved from her bedroom her tin of sewing widgets and the lap frame as well.

Colt garnered a thimble from a package of assorted sizes and shed his tie. He propelled the quilting needle with the thimble and tunneled the point toward himself, gathering stitches.

Paula's hair grazed his cheek as she leaned in to verify she was seeing what she thought she was seeing. His lashes caught the light in their upward arc. Battling rogue memories of times past when touching had been savored, sweet and deliberate, she focused on his stitches. "Very nice. You've had some practice."

"When push came to shove, a stint at the quilting frame was Mom's spin on time-out." Colt's gray eyes glimmered at the memory.

"Who'd you push?" asked Paula.

"C.J. When he wasn't pushing *me,*" Colt said.

Seeing his mouth twitch opened another floodgate. Paula got to her feet and crossed to adjust the air-conditioning.

"I can hear Mom as if it were yesterday. 'Keep your hands to yourself, Colton Jacob,'" Colt was saying.

"Colton *Jacob?*" interrupted Joy. She tipped her face. "You and Uncle C.J. have the same first name?"

Colt nodded. "Colton was my mother's maiden name."

Joy made a curious face that bespoke the voids in her knowledge of Colt's side of her family. "Tell me about my grandparents."

"Sure. But first, thread yourself a needle, and help me out here," suggested Colt.

"I don't know how," admitted Joy.

"You can learn, can't you?" he challenged.

In the past, Paula had tried to interest Joy in sewing. Having failed at it, she was surprised to find Joy reaching for a needle.

Paula put on some music as Colt set about teaching Joy. Once Joy had learned the basics, he talked Paula into joining them. It was close quarters, complicated by Colt's injured leg resting on the bulky ottoman.

Paula sat facing Colt. She started her needle on his side of the frame, working it back toward herself while he started his needle on her side of the frame and did the same. They traded needles and repeated the process.

Joy's interest in needlework quickly waned. But her curiosity about Colt was insatiable. While his responses to her questions fell short of filling in the missing years, they did shed light on his professional life as an investigative reporter. Paula had been mistaken in assuming his scars were recent. As it turned out, he had received them years earlier while investigating some unsavory characters who were now serving time in a federal penitentiary.

"One man had guard dogs. Well-trained ones," Colt added.

"They attacked you? Yikes." Wide-eyed, Joy asked, "Were the men gangsters?"

"No. Just a couple of good old boys gone bad. How's your online schooling coming along?" Colt changed the subject.

"I aced my creative writing test. My computer's on. If you're up to it, come on and I'll show you," urged Joy.

In their wake, Paula moved into the sunlight

flooding through the window. At length, Colt returned alone and crossed to the window on his crutches. Paula glanced up from her quilting and found him looking on over her shoulder.

"Where's Joy?"

"She's finishing up something she's writing, then she's off for a swim," he replied.

Joy sailed out of her room a short while later. Clad in a tangerine-colored swimsuit and matching sandals, she beckoned to Colt with a bejeweled finger. "Come sit in the sunshine, Dad."

"Maybe I'll settle for what's coming through the window instead," he replied.

Joy shot her parents an appraising glance that grew into a sly smile. She went her way, sandals slapping out a perky beat.

The pool was in full view of the window. Responding to his gentle chuckle, Paula asked, "What's she up to now?"

"Come see."

Paula shuttled the quilt and frame aside. She joined Colt at the window to find Joy orchestrating a game of follow the leader off the diving board.

"That's my Joy. Never met a child she couldn't coerce into playing with her."

As Paula looked on, Joy executed a clumsy belly flop off the board.

"Ouch! That's gotta smart." Colt chuckled. "Better teach her how to tuck her head and go in clean."

"She knows how. She's testing their mettle."

Together, they laughed as five kids followed suit, smacking the water one by one. The perfect jackknife Joy executed next was a good deal harder for the other children to copy.

"Say! She's pretty good," said Colt.

Hearing the pride Joy's dive had surprised in him, Paula felt the tug of a bond as yet unexplored. The accompanying tenderness caught her off guard. Paula withdrew to her chair. But Colt lingered at the window, watching Joy. A hush fell between them. He remained there a long while.

So long, Paula was about to offer him a chair when he eased out a weary sigh and hobbled back to the sofa. The simple act of lowering himself to the cushions was an effort for a man on crutches. Shifting his injured leg to the ottoman appeared to be a job, too. And painful. He winced as he did so.

"Would you like a pillow for your foot?" asked Paula.

"No, thanks. I'm comfortable," he claimed.

Paula snipped off a new length of thread and pushed it through the eye of her needle. "You were limping before that car struck you. A previous injury, they said at the hospital. Was that career-related, too?"

"I like an assignment with some edge to it," he conceded.

Paula watched him pass a hand over his scarred face. She was beginning to recognize the gesture as habitual. "So you've made a life of putting yourself in harm's way for a by-line?"

"Asks the woman who services high-rise signs for a living."

"Jake and his crew do the sky work. I'm too claustrophobic to be much use at working behind sign faces," Paula admitted.

"So what's your niche?"

"I bend neon, answer the phone and keep books."

Colt's smile warmed his worn demeanor. "Does that make you upper management?"

"That would be Jake. I've got enough to do, raising Joy."

"You've done a fine job. Though you might want to address that willful streak of hers. Did she get that from you?"

"Oh, sure. Blame it on me!"

Mingled laughter eased into a harmonious silence as Paula resumed quilting. The ticking of the nearby clock accompanied the whisper of thread through cotton layers. The refrigerator hummed in the galley kitchen. Music droned softly in the background.

At length, Paula looked to see Colt's eyes drifting shut. Her muscles had grown stiff from sitting so long. She shifted her head first to one side, then the other.

"Stiff neck?" Colt spoke up.

"Shoulders, too," she admitted. "Did I wake you?"

"I wasn't asleep. Just resting my eyes."

Colt hobbled onto his crutches and circled behind her armchair. By the time Paula ascertained his intention, it was awkward to protest.

Colt kneaded with one hand the tender place at the base of her neck.

Her skin heated to his hands. "That's good. Thanks," she murmured and sat forward.

Colt supported his weight against the back of the chair, freeing both hands in an effort to give her stiff muscles his full attention. His thumbs were strong and unerring, his fingers intuitive as they moved over her shoulders and upper back.

Like a sanding block in a carpenter's palm, his hands made dust of Paula's composure. Every nuance of his scent—his soap, his shaving cream, the spice of his cologne—evoked memories. She came to her feet so quickly, the quilt and frame tumbled out of her lap. Tangling her feet in them, she fought for her balance on every level.

"Steady there!" cautioned Colt, reaching over the chair to lend his support. "You okay?"

"I'm fine." Face averted, Paula swept the quilt and frame from the floor. "You're free to run along home now."

"I beg your pardon?"

"Just go!" Paula wheeled to face him with a fiery glance.

Colt's startled expression shifted to one more discerning. Like a shadow passing over a field, perception gave way to silent compliance. He got his crutches beneath him and hobbled to the connecting door before turning back to meet her harried demeanor.

"What is it now?"

"About these mood swings of yours…" he began.

"Mood swings?" Emotional rope unraveling, Paula countered, "You're calling *me* moody?"

"Yesterday, you were all thistles. Your chin climbed a little higher every time I opened my mouth. This morning, you were the sweet woman I've carried in my memory all these years. About the time I decide you've had a change of heart toward me, the wind shifts."

"Oh. So you're upset because I asked you to leave."

"I'm not upset. I'm confused. What is it you want from me, anyway?"

"I want you to keep your word, Colton!"

Paula lowered stinging eyes. "We agreed to be very careful with Joy, did we not?"

"Your rules, and yes, I did agree," he admitted. "I didn't have much choice if I wanted to spend time with my daughter."

"Exactly! And nothing's changed," Paula retorted, "So just keep your hands to yourself, all right?"

"I will. I'm sorry if I offended you," he added.

"Forget it." Paula wanted to let the whole subject die a quick death.

A silent plea darkened his pewter-colored eyes as he searched her face. His hand moved over his scars again. His lips parted, and still he paused, as if choosing his words with great care. "Could I say one more thing?"

"About what?"

"About us."

"There is no us."

"Maybe not now. But if the weather should change and the temperature should rise…"

"Go home, Colt. Please?" she pleaded.

"Just humor me. What's the harm in rethinking it?" he coaxed softly.

Paula bit her tongue to keep from being

softened by his powers of persuasion. They traded a long glance, his tinged in regrets. His crutches, padded though they were, echoed across the floor of her heart like tramping feet.

Hot, isn't it? She had only to say it and even now, he would turn back with the anticipated response. And then what? Paula raked a hand through her hair, torn even as the connecting door latched behind Colt. She locked it on her side. It was a good deal harder to lock down awakened desires that had slumbered so long, she had relegated them to her past.

It left her shaken. Not the fact that she had desires. But that Colt could still awaken them. The one who had battered and beaten her heart could not only hurt her feelings, but evoke a physical response. Sweet woman, indeed! *Fool me once, shame on you. Fool me twice, shame on me.*

Too restless to sit and quilt, Paula went outdoors. Seeing her, Joy climbed out of the pool.

''Where's Dad?'' she asked.

''He went to his room. My guess is he's resting.''

''Can I go see?''

Paula started to discourage her, then gave it up. "Put on some dry clothes first."

Joy bid her new friends goodbye and went inside. She had showered and changed by the time Paula returned to her quilting. But Colt didn't answer Joy's knock.

Disappointed, Joy retreated. "I'll be in my room, if he calls."

When the call came, it was a dinner invitation that included Paula. But wisdom dictated otherwise. Paula went for a walk instead. Along the way, she paced back over the years, trying to connect with the woman-child she had been when she first began mooning over a billboard, little knowing that handsome image would materialize into the flesh-and-blood man of her dreams.

But how could the power of that attraction span a dozen-plus lonely years and bushwhack her all over again?

Unable to explain her churning emotions Paula stopped for a bite to eat, then resumed her walk, arriving back at the lodge at dusk.

She settled in the tub for a long soak in lavender-scented water, then dressed for bed and crawled between the sheets to decompress with a suspense novel by her favorite Christian author.

But it wasn't the story line running through her mind as she turned out the lamp and curled her arm around her pillow.

It was Colt's soft plea, "What's the harm in rethinking it?"

Was he bidding for reconciliation? If so, why? Did he still have feelings for her? Or was reconciliation a sacrifice he was willing to make in exchange for the chance to be an everyday father to Joy?

Chapter Eleven

Long after Mrs. Hilbert had come and gone, Colt lay awake, thinking about the sermon he'd heard that day:

> For as high as the heavens are above the earth, so great is His love for those who fear Him; as far as the east is from the west, so far has He removed our transgressions from us. As a father has compassion on his children, so the Lord has compassion on those who fear Him for He knows how we are formed, He remembers that we are dust.

Dust. The taste of it was in Colt's mouth. He couldn't erase from his mind Paula's strug-

gling against tears as she implored him to keep
his word.

He reviewed as he had so many times in the
past his abandonment of Paula, though at the
time he would not have used that term. He had
been so certain their marriage was doomed.
Leaving her was the hardest thing he had ever
done. Was it truly a noble sacrifice? Or self-
deception? Joy bore the scars of a missing parent. Paula, the burden of single parenting. *And
what of him?* Loss. Loss. Loss.

The Gideon Bible from the bedside table lay
open to the verses spoken in church. "As far
as the east is from the west, so far as He removed our transgressions from us." The words
glistened on the page like cool water from the
hand of a loving friend. A pardon that wiped
the wrong from memory, while humanly impossible, was promised by God.

The wave of longing flooding Colt surpassed
the leaden ache of his injuries. Stretched out on
the bed, he shielded his eyes from the glaring
lamp. But the eyes of his heart were wide-open
to God's word as he prayed, asking and receiv-

ing forgiveness, a pardon that not only forgave but forgot. Exhaustion eventually claimed him.

The lamp was still on when the phone awoke him at daybreak. It was Walt Snyder, checking in. Colt got his bearings, and told him about Paula's exchange with the pastor in the hospital elevator.

Walt didn't bother with office hours. He called Reed Custer at home, then reported back. Colt thought about knocking on Paula's door to share what Walt had related. But she had an attitude where Monique was concerned. Anyway, after asking him to leave yesterday, she had locked her door behind him, a gesture that spoke louder than words.

Joy was already up and at the computer tackling her schoolwork when Paula got out of bed.

Paula kissed her cheek. "Good girl. I'm off for my morning walk."

"Take your time. Dad's right next door," said Joy.

As if she needed reminding. Paula donned a long skirt and floral-print jacket over a pale-yellow shell. Her walk took her past the Biblical garden.

Inexplicably drawn, she let herself in through the open gate and continued along the garden path toward a gazebo. Screened as it was by yellow roses and other vining plants, she was almost upon the gazebo before she saw the bench within it was occupied. Her breath caught in her throat.

"Colt! You gave me a start," said Paula. "How'd you get here?"

"Mrs. Hilbert dropped me off. But I'm hoping to hoof it back." Colt folded the New Testament from which he had been reading into his pocket. "I talked to Walt a bit ago. Care to join me?"

"Is there news?" asked Paula.

"Of a sort," replied Colt. "When I mentioned your meeting a pastor in the hospital elevator, and that the timing coincided with Joy's scare, Walt called Reed Custer at home."

"And?" prompted Paula.

"Reed *was* at the hospital that morning. He wasn't sure of the time. And here's the clincher—he always takes the stairs for exercise."

Paula dropped down on the bench like a lead balloon. "So it wasn't him."

"No."

"So we're back to square one. Was the guy I talked to really a pastor? Or someone pretending to be."

"Exactly," said Colt. "Walt plans to touch base with Detective Browning this morning. As for Reed, he offered to contact a couple of the people who volunteer their time at Can-Do Mission."

Puzzled, Paula tipped her face. "I don't understand. What do volunteers at a homeless shelter have to do with what happened at the hospital?"

"Nothing," said Colt. "But there's an outside chance one of them may have a line on Monique."

"Her again," said Paula.

"She's the key to seeing justice done where Simon Burwell is concerned," replied Colt. "Of the volunteers, she was closest to a guy by the name of Patrick Delaney. That's who paid her way so she could attend the retreat. Incidentally, Walt says Delaney was engaged to Jake's fiancée for a while."

"Oh, *that* Delaney."

"Then you do know him?"

"Not personally. Just that he jilted Shelby and left her holding prepaid honeymoon reservations at Wildwood."

"Wildwood?" echoed Colt.

Paula nodded. "It's a local resort. Shelby drove down intending to spend what would have been her honeymoon writing. That didn't pan out either. But that's another story. Back to Delaney—are you thinking Monique may have confided her whereabouts to him?"

"It's a long shot, but Walt's going to check," said Colt. "I can't be sure Monique's in hiding, mind you. But I prefer to think she has stayed a step ahead of Burwell, and that she may even be able to offer information key to finding him. I'd sure like to see this whole matter wrapped up without any more violence."

Sobered by the realization that the exact opposite could be true, that Monique could have become a victim of her ex-husband's vengeance, Paula closed her eyes.

"The saffron crocus are in bloom. See there?" said Colt as if he, too, needed to absorb the tranquility of this garden retreat.

Paula opened her eyes to admire the garble of autumn crocus covertly tucked amidst other late bloomers and varied greens. A fountain trickled nearby. A flag swayed in the air overhead. Birds warbled resilient songs. The sights and scents and affable sounds were little pockets of resistance on the downcast face of gritty realities.

Colt maneuvered to his crutches. "Let's walk, shall we?"

The talk was small as they strolled past pungent junipers, a young pine and a sturdy cedar sapling. The trees were skirted by herbs and autumn flowers and grain-bearing field flowers, all sharing common ground.

"Such a variety of plants growing together in harmony," mused Paula.

"Makes you wonder, why can't we?"

Paula faltered at Colt's hushed reply. Leaning on one crutch, he plucked a yellow rose and held it out to her. "Peace offering."

"For what?" she asked, taking it.

"Getting too close yesterday."

"I thought we'd agreed to forget that."

"I'm trying." Colt drew a shallow breath as she hid her face in the rose. "Is yellow still your favorite?"

"Yes," she said, and thanked him. "Though we probably shouldn't be helping ourselves."

"I can put it back if you like," he offered.

Paula's mouth curved. She turned the rose between her fingers, and raised it to her face. "Smells almost as good as if we'd come by it honestly."

He chuckled and changed the subject. "What can you tell me about this story Joy's writing?"

"The one Shelby gave her?"

"Yes. She wants me to collaborate on it with her."

"Oh, she does, does she? Did she also tell you she initially read the story without Shelby's knowledge?"

Colt rested on his crutches. "Before Shelby turned it over to her?"

"I'm afraid so. I suspect it was intended as a peace offering on Shelby's part." A sigh escaped Paula. "Joy plays a poor second fiddle."

"She was jealous of Shelby?" Colt proved intuitive.

Paula nodded. "I should have seen it coming. Jake's been like a father to her."

It was a phrase Paula had used repeatedly over the years, a rosette she hung on Jake. This time, it came at Colt's expense. She saw him flinch. Regretting her carelessness, she apologized. "That was tactless. I'm sorry."

"For telling the truth? Don't be," said Colt. "I'm indebted to Jake for being there."

Paula's remorse clucked and clattered like a rock caught in a hubcap. The idle conversation that carried them to the garden gate was heavily polite. Pausing to open it, she asked, "How's your leg holding up?"

"Doing fine, thanks. Have you had breakfast yet?"

"I didn't take time," she admitted.

"Let's grab a bite on our way back, shall we?"

A little sidewalk diner down the street proved a timely rest stop between the church and the lodge. Paula's plucking nerves quieted over a hearty breakfast. Lingering over coffee, Colt spoke of his as yet unfinished article on Simon Burwell. Which brought the conversation back to Monique and his hopes that she might provide a link to her ex-husband.

"As bitter as she was over all Simon had put her through, I think she'd be more than happy to help the police locate him for questioning, if we could just find her.''

"Talk about love going awry!" said Paula.

"A little like us?" he offered.

Paula looked up from her tepid coffee. "I'm not bitter. And I don't want a fight." Struggling to be honest, she added, "Single parenting is no picnic. Joy and I have had some problems. And not just with Shelby."

"How do you mean?" asked Colt.

Paula looked back over the past summer, remembering how threatened she felt as her relationship with Joy deteriorated. Colt had made a tempting target. Repenting of her biased view, she admitted, "There are voids in her life that I can't fill. Neither can Jake."

"Dad spaces?" he eased the way.

Nodding, Paula found it easier to admit than she would have a week earlier. "Joy tells me you two are going to the water park this afternoon," she said in prelude to the long awaited topic of shared custody.

"That's the plan. You're welcome to join us," he invited.

"Thanks. It sounds like fun. But, if there's

any hope of ever finishing Joy's quilt, I need to stay on track.''

Colt gave it a moment's study. ''If I help you with the quilt this morning, would that free you up your afternoon?''

''That's generous of you, Colt. I appreciate the offer. But I'm not sure Joy will welcome my tagging along,'' said Paula.

''Then again, she might. Wouldn't hurt to ask,'' Colt added.

His coaxing found a receptive audience. Quieting her doubts, Paula agreed to do so. Together, they returned to the lodge. Colt had a message from Walt, asking him to call.

In so doing, he learned that Detective Browning was going over a list of pastors who made regular calls at the hospital.

''I gave him Paula's description of the man in the elevator,'' continued Walt. ''He'll do some checking in hopes of finding the guy. But we'll have to be patient, it'll take some time.''

''What about Delaney?'' asked Colt.

''Nothing so far. I haven't been able to reach him.''

Colt related the news to Paula as they worked

on the quilt. The remainder of the morning passed quickly.

Joy finished her schoolwork in time to join them for lunch. "I'm glad you're coming with us, Mom. Suit up, and we'll do the water slide together."

Pleased by Joy's reaction, Paula slipped into her swimsuit and pulled a green seersucker gingham sundress on over it. She filled a cooler with chilled soft drinks and packed snacks as well.

The park was only a short drive from the lodge. Colt found a shady spot and settled there. Paula explored the water attractions with Joy until a group of home-schoolers about Joy's age lured her away.

Paula neared the umbrella-shaded redwood table where Colt was enjoying his small patch of shade. He looked up from his book, past her to Joy and her newfound friends. "You've been replaced?"

"Handily so. I was ready for soda and some sunscreen, anyway," said Paula, reaching for her sunglasses.

He chuckled and passed her a soft drink, but

couldn't find the sunscreen. "Would you settle for some shade instead?" he asked.

"If I could find some."

"Pull up a chair here beside me, slant the umbrella a bit and you'll have it."

Paula accepted his invitation. Tilting the umbrella so it shaded them both, she draped a towel over her shoulders and fetched her book from the mesh bag she had brought along. But the novel didn't hold her attention.

Perhaps Colt's book wasn't up to par, either. He put it aside. Lounging side by side, they idled away the afternoon, Joy-watching and meandering down shared tributaries of memory lane, then upstream beyond where their lives had branched.

In response to Paula's interest, Colt described his refurbished vintage twenties apartment. He likened the high tin ceilings and handsome crown moldings to those he remembered from her parents' home in Liberty Flats. Paula confessed her sorrow over the deteriorating condition of the old home place. Like Gram's house, it had been built by her grandfather. Unlike Gram's, it had changed hands numerous times over the past dozen years and now sat vacant and in very bad repair.

"Ripe for a restoration, eh?" said Colt.

"Or the wrecking ball," said Paula. "Joy says we should rescue it. Not that we need that much house. Nor could we beg, borrow or steal enough cash to do it justice. Anyway, I'm content with our house. It's just the right size for two people with busy lives and little time for mop and polish."

The afternoon shadows grew long. Joy bid her friends goodbye and complained of being famished. As they gathered their belongings, Colt suggested a cookout. Paula seconded the motion, then yielded to Joy's pleas for a snack and stopped for an Ogle dog. The crusty batter-dipped hot dog smelled tempting. But both Paula and Colt held out for steaks.

Finding a general store wedged between a T-shirt shop and an art studio where old-time mountain crafts were plied, Paula chose thick cuts and trimmings for the grill. She tucked a ready-made salad into her basket and a half gallon of peach ice cream for dessert.

Joy found handmade candles for the terrace table. The yellow roses caught Colt's eye. He bought a dozen and let Joy pick the vase. She settled on a large hand-turned pottery vessel on which hearts had been fashioned as adornment.

It was dark by the time they gathered around Paula's terrace table for a late dinner. The sliding glass door leading into Colt's suite was open as well. His ringing phone interrupted the blessing. Joy bolted up and away to answer it. She returned a moment later to report that Mrs. Hilbert wanted Colt to know she might be a little late.

"It's her twenty-fifth wedding anniversary," Joy explained as she reclaimed her place at the table. "She and her husband are going to grab a bite to eat before she comes."

"I wish I'd known. I could have invited them to have dinner with us," said Paula.

"For their anniversary? No way! They should go somewhere fancy," said Joy. "With dancing afterward. And a carriage ride under the stars. That would be romantic."

"Did you see your quilt, Joy? We're coming along nicely." Paula sought to get Joy off the romance track.

"I've got a finger that's starting to feel like sandpaper." Colt followed suit.

"From feeling for the needle from the bottom side." Paula nodded. "Me, too."

"Let me see." Joy reached simultaneously for both Paula's and Colt's hands. "Pincushion fingers. Matched set. What do ya know?" She sandwiched their hands, fingertips to fingertips. Holding them between her open palms, she sang a line from an old Beatles hand-holding classic.

In no hurry to retrieve his hand, Colt chortled, "Where'd you hear that one?"

"Gram Kate's. She has a whole set of old forty-fives. Why? Was it your song? Yours and Mom's when you were dating, I mean?"

"We're not quite old." Paula pulled her hand away, and sought once more to sidetrack Joy. "How's your steak?"

"Delicious. You're a good cook, Mom. Don't you think, Dad?"

"I certainly do," said Colt. He smiled at Paula. "I don't know when I've enjoyed a home-cooked meal more."

Joy grinned like a cat in a sunny window. She parked her elbows on the table, and rested her chin on steepled fingers. "Maybe I won't be a writer after all. Maybe I'll be a marriage doctor when I grow up.''

''Elbows off the table, Joy,'' said Paula. Passing Colt a dish of peas, pearl onions and mushrooms, she voiced her hopes of getting an early start in the morning. ''I'd like to get my morning walk in. Then I'm going to settle in and quilt.''

''If you want some help, I'm free,'' offered Colt.

''Great!'' Thinking of Gram's old adage about many hands making light work, Paula said, ''With your help, I think we can finish the quilting by noon.''

''I'll specialize in arranging nice getaways for all my patients,'' said Joy.

''I need to make up my mind about the binding.'' Paula refused to acknowledge Joy's pointing like a bird dog on the scent.

''I was wondering how you planned to finish it,'' said Colt.

Paula voiced a couple of ideas, including packaged binding.

''Would you *listen* to yourselves?'' Joy rolled her eyes. ''You'll have to start another

quilt the minute you finish mine, or you won't
have a thing to talk about!''

"Is this the marriage doctor practicing without license again?" asked Colt.

"It is," countered Joy. "And might I suggest
you make this one a wedding quilt?"

"Give it a rest." Paula fired a quiet warning.

"For Uncle Jake and Shelby, I mean." Joy
covered her verbal backside.

"Or how about this? You wrap up Shelby's
story and return it as a wedding gift," suggested Colt evenly.

Joy jerked her head around. "Huh?"

"She may like another shot at it," said Colt.

Joy's face fell. "Give it back? You can't be
serious?"

"I wouldn't joke about your keeping something that doesn't belong to you," said Colt.

"It *does* belong to me. Shelby gave it to
me!" sputtered Joy.

"Under a cloud of suspicion, as I understand
it."

"Why? What did Mom tell you?"

Intercepting the thundercloud expression Joy
aimed at Paula, Colt said, "Leave your mother
out of it. This is your father telling you that if

you're serious about being a writer, you need to come up with your own ideas and follow through with them. If you have a problem with that, feel free to say so.''

Wounded tears sprang to Joy's eyes. Blinking them back, she glowered at them both. ''Talk about getting ganged up on!''

''Yes, well you might want to keep that in mind and adjust your agenda accordingly,'' said Colt.

Failing to see any humor in that suggestion, Joy's mouth turned down in a sulky pout. ''Does that mean you're going to *make* me give back Shelby's story?''

''I'm offering advice,'' replied Colt. ''Do what you will with it.''

Watching Colt's face, Joy caught her lip, and held her silence a long moment. When she spoke again, it was to quietly ask, ''Will you be mad if I keep it?''

''No. But then I've been disappointed before,'' said Colt.

Joy looked stricken. But relief lifted Paula's heart by the bootstraps. Mountain-moving relief swam through her at the realization she had nothing to fear in Colt. Far from it. She had found an ally in him, and was grateful for his gentle handling of the whole situation.

His gaze was warm as he thanked her for dinner and reached for his crutches. "It was delicious. Thank you for including me, Paula."

"I bought ice cream for dessert," she reminded him.

"Maybe another time. I believe I'll go dial up a florist and have some flowers waiting for Mrs. Hilbert when she arrives."

"For her anniversary? How sweet." Thinking to spare him some trouble, Paula indicated the roses Colt had arranged in the center of the table. "If you'd like, you're welcome to these."

"Thanks, but those are taken. I picked them with you in mind," replied Colt.

"Yellow, I noticed." Paula stretched a hand toward a velvet petal. "They're lovely. As was the gesture. Thank you."

There was a boyish quality to the quiet pleasure expressed in his smile. Paula's skin warmed. She lowered her flushing face to the roses. "There's a florist a couple of blocks down. Maybe Joy would go fetch you a bouquet."

"I'd appreciate it," chimed Colt. "Unless you'd rather stay and do the dishes, Joy."

Joy slumped deeper into her chair. "Dishes."

"Joy," murmured Paula at her refractory muttering.

"It's all right. I'll handle it by phone." Balanced on his crutches, Colt paused behind Paula's chair, and gave her shoulder a reassuring pat.

Paula swallowed her reprimand for Joy. Even more disturbing than Joy's bad manners were the sensations radiating from the warm imprint Colt's passing touch had left. In his wake, she was surprised to find tears standing in Joy's eyes. "What's the matter?"

"Dad's mean. Serve him right if I just gave up and let you two be miserable the rest of your lives."

"Oh, Joy. Grow up," said Paula absently. She cradled a single rose blossom with her cupped hand and inhaled its sweet fragrance. Feeling sun-washed even in the midst of Joy's little tempest, she started inside.

"Where are you going?" Joy called after her.

"Mrs. Hilbert's due any time. Your father's

going to have a hard time finding a florist quick enough for the job.''

''So you're going for him?''

''I thought I'd offer.'' Turning back, she saw Joy's expression shift to a grudging smirk. Knowing how much Joy despised doing dishes, she added, ''Unless you've changed your mind, and would like to go while I do the dishes.''

''No, thanks,'' said Joy.

Paula let herself in through the terrace door, cut through their quarters and rapped on Colt's door. There was no answer. She knocked again.

''Colt?'' she called and tried the knob. It turned unchecked. The door swung open. The lamplight burning within poured a soft glow into the shadows. But Colt wasn't in view.

Hearing a crashing and a muffled outcry from deeper within the apartment, Paula bolted toward the sound to find Colt facedown on the bedroom floor.

Chapter Twelve

Paula plunged to her haunches beside Colt. "Colt! What happened?" she bleated.

"This blamed leg." Colt lifted his chin off the plush carpet and winced in helpless frustration.

"Are you hurt? How'd you fall?" cried Paula.

"My medicine bottle rolled under the bed. I tried to fish it out with my crutch."

"I'll get help." Paula sprang to her feet.

Colt gripped her ankle to prevent her from doing so. "That's not necessary. I can get up. Just get a hand under my shoulder and the other one under my right hip and help me roll to my side, would you please?''

Paula's eyes dimmed with doubt. ''Are you sure?''

''Trust me. All I need is a hand up,'' insisted Colt.

Reluctantly, Paula assented and got her hands beneath him.

''That's right. Are you ready?'' asked Colt.

At her nod, Colt rolled to his left side, curled and planted his right leg behind his outstretched left leg. It served as an anchor to keep him from rolling on over to his back.

''I don't think this is a good idea,'' hedged Paula.

''It'll be fine. Nothing hurt but my pride.'' Fearing she would change her mind and back out, Colt prodded, ''Get your arms under mine, would you please?''

Paula ceased protesting. She got behind him and used her arms like scoops.

''Don't lift, I'm too heavy for you,'' cautioned Colt. ''Just help me keep my balance.''

With Paula steadying him, Colt moved from his side to a seated position with his legs stretched out in front of him. "Now get me a chair."

Paula fetched a sturdy wooden relic from beneath the window. She set the chair down against the bed, parallel to his upper body with the chair seat facing him.

"Perfect." Colt gripped the seat, preparing to lever himself up. But Paula's hands shot out to delay him.

"Wait a second! I'm not sure I can catch you if you start to go down."

"No, and don't you try," he warned. "Just stand back, okay?"

One moment, Paula was hovering over him, worried. The next she hunkered down behind him, her arms around his waist, sending little shock waves through him.

"I said—"

"I heard you." Her sudden sharpness cut through his objections. "If you're going to ignore common sense precautions, then just do it and be done with it, would you please?"

Colt set his jaw and marshaled his strength, wanting to spare her. But beneath all that feminine softness, she was strong and steady. With her help, he went from his forearms to his palms in one fluid motion, then straightened his arms and pulled himself upright and onto his good leg. Balanced there, strength rapidly waning, he rasped, ''Shove the chair out of the way, would you please?''

Paula shifted with one arm still around him, and pushed the chair aside with her foot. Leaning on her shoulder, Colt eased around and gingerly lowered himself to the edge of the bed.

''Your color's dreadful,'' Paula said flatly. ''You're in pain. I can tell just by looking. I'm calling the hotel's doctor.''

But Colt intercepted her hand as she reached for the bedside extension. ''My leg's complaining a little, that's all. No need to panic. It'll quit, once I get my foot up.''

''Then lie down. We'll prop it up and if that doesn't do the trick, I'm getting some professional help.'' Paula tossed the pillows to one side and turned back the bedcovers. ''Ready?''

Colt set his jaw, hesitant to tell her that he wasn't sure he could lift his own foot. His leg felt as if it were on fire. But Paula anticipated his need. Her gentle hands supported his injured leg. It minimized the jostling as Colt stretched out on the bed. He wiped cold sweat from his

brow and eased out a sigh of weary relief.
"Good thing you came along."

"You should go to the hospital just to be on
the safe side," she chided.

"No need. A good night's rest, and I'll be
good as new."

His trumped-up confidence did little to
lighten her concern. But she stopped short of
insisting, and put a pillow under his foot.

"Better?" she asked.

"Yes, thanks," said Colt. In truth, the throbbing in his leg was now synchronizing with his
swift-beating heart.

Paula retrieved a second pillow for his head.
"Up you go."

A lock of her hair brushed his face as she
eased the pillow beneath his head. He lifted a
hand as if to capture the tress, then caught himself and arrested the motion midair.

Her cheeks blazed a brighter hue. Her blue
gaze held his, a light burning there, too. Something old, something new. But tenuous and vulnerable, like a fragile shoot trying to find its
way around a garden stone.

Colt guarded his own reaction and said, "I
owe you one."

"Actually, I came to thank you," she murmured.

"You did? For what?" He pushed past his own dazedness at her hovering face and soft rosy hue.

"Taking Joy in hand. About Shelby's book," Paula added.

"Oh, the story-gifting." It was the furthest thing from Colt's mind. He watched her lashes come down.

"On the one hand, I didn't want to discourage Joy's interest in writing. But I worried it sent the wrong message, and that Shelby might come to regret her generosity," she said carefully. "Particularly, if Joy got in the middle again. With Jake, I mean. Though that seems a lot less likely, now that you're in her life."

Taken aback in the most pleasant of ways, Colt inserted, "That's good to know."

"I caved, Colt," she admitted with sudden abandon. "I took the easy way out. I couldn't put myself through making her give it back. She took it much better, coming from you."

"It's only fair. You shouldn't have to take the heat all the time," he soothed.

A red tress fell across her face. Their hands

collided as each reached to smooth it into submission. Her hands were quicker and better trained. His mouth lifted to see her flick the errant lock behind her shell-shaped ear.

She smiled back, lips parting in a color-washed face. Her expression was tender. Her eyes gleamed. Colt's twittering leg pulsated, a deep bass beat in a symphony of sweet yearning. The air thickened. His throat did, too.

"Warm in here, isn't it?" he rumbled.

"I'll adjust the air," she offered.

But he forestalled her with a soft sound and a square-tipped finger that came to rest in the hollow of her throat. He longed to seal that hollow with his kiss and move on to refresh his memory regarding all that he had surrendered rights to years earlier.

Her lips were an invitation, moist and irresistibly tipped. He touched his mouth to hers and wonder of wonders, found invitation. Heard it in her swift intake of breath and saw it in the eyes that met his. Lost in those morning glory pools, he rumbled, "Maybe it's not the heat, maybe it's the humidity."

"You think?"

Laughter rose in him, surprised delight at her

response. She answered with a sound from her throat that went over him in a throbbing tempo, scattering gooseflesh. He collected another tenuous kiss, caught his fingers in her hair. "You're a good nurse. An angel in disguise," he whispered. "Did I remember to say thank you?"

"Is that you or your painkillers talking?" she asked, her lips close to his.

He chuckled at her coy glance. "They're antibiotics. And they're still under the bed."

"Now might be a good time for me to get them for you, don't you think?"

His heart checked its mad race. He memorized the touch of her supple fingers, and suffered loss as she withdrew them. "Have I offended you?" he asked.

In lieu of an answer, she retrieved the pill bottle from beneath his bed. Colt forgot to breathe as he watched her set it down on the nightstand. Her fingers trailed over the framed picture resting there. It was one Joy had sent him of herself last summer. She was standing on the grassy roadside, looking up at a billboard image of a guy who bore little resemblance to the man Colt faced in the mirror each morning.

A scarless fellow, inside and out, air-brushed to perfection.

Following Paula's gaze, his voice turned to husk. "What then? Is it the scars?"

Her face clouded that he should ask. "I'd forgotten them."

"But now that I've reminded you—is it something you can't get past?" he pressed.

Hurt floated up from those bottomless pools. "Does it matter?"

The stirring in his chest seemed to tug with each labored breath. "It does to me. I'd like to think you still feel something when we touch. Or is that a lie I'm telling myself?"

Averting her face, she picked up the picture, and pressed a finger to Joy's image. "There's more involved than your feelings and mine."

"Whose, then? Joy's? The marriage doctor's?" Almost afraid to believe that her concern for Joy's well-being was all that stood between them, Colt entreated, "Are you kidding? She'd be over the moon if she knew we were having this conversation."

"She's a child, Colt. She hasn't a clue as to the difficulties."

"Maybe not. But she knows what she wants.

She's been pushing for this from the moment she stepped foot into my hospital room. She wanted to know did I still love you and would I like some help." Colt heard her breath catch.

"What did you tell her?"

"To mind her own business. Or something to that effect."

"But now you're bowing to her wishes," she said quietly.

Her words were clear enough, yet seemingly contradictory. Confused, he asked, "And the error in that is…?"

"If you have to ask, then maybe we both need some time to rest on this."

She searched his face for what, he didn't know. He knew only that it was a fruitless quest. Her eyes lost their luster. The fire cooled. Her lashes came down. Even before she moved away, hope sputtered low.

"I'll get you a glass of water so you can take your pills," she said on her way out.

Was she afraid? Unsure of the next step? Or simply unwilling to take it? Like a bird tearing up his nest, Colt searched for an explanation. The telephone jarred him with its shrillness.

"Do you want me to answer that?" Paula called from the next room.

"If you don't mind." Colt grasped at straws in hopes of detaining her that they might talk further.

He backtracked over the conversation, searching even as Paula returned with his water and the portable phone. Her gaze glanced off the extension on his nightstand within easy reach.

"It's Walt Snyder." She gave him the phone. "What about the flowers? Did you call?"

"Yes, the shop down the street agreed to make up a bouquet. It seemed simpler to have it delivered to Mrs. Hilbert's home. I was going to look up her address right after I took my pills."

"Why don't I just pick up the flowers for you?" Paula offered.

"You don't mind?"

"Not at all," she said.

Hoping to resume where they had left off and discern what had caused her to shut down emotionally, Colt accepted her offer. "Thanks, Paula. Hurry back," he called after her.

Walt's call proved to be good news. The police had picked up for questioning a man by the name of Lefty Banks in connection with driving the car that had struck Colt and fled the scene.

"Any priors?" asked Colt.

"A long list," replied Walt.

"What about threatening Joy? Could he be responsible for that, too?"

"I'm afraid not, Colt. Banks couldn't have been at the hospital that day. He was in court on unrelated charges at the time," said Walt.

Colt massaged the dull pain radiating from his thigh. "What about the pastor in the elevator? Have the police had any luck finding him?"

"Not yet. His identity is still a mystery," said Walt. "At this point, I'd say he's the most likely suspect where your daughter's concerned. Though I can't figure out his motive in threatening her."

It puzzled Colt, too, and had all along. Briefly Walt brought Colt up to speed on other details of the investigation. They were still talking when Paula tiptoed in and set the anniversary bouquet down on his bedside table.

"Lovely!" Colt mouthed the word, then covered the receiver with his hand, protesting,

"Wait a second, Paula. Don't run off. I want to talk to you."

"I can't stay. Mrs. Hilbert pulled in just behind me." Backing away from his bedside, Paula lifted her hand in a parting wave.

"I'll call you later, then. Thanks!" Colt called after her.

She shot him a wordless smile over her shoulder, and let herself out.

Mrs. Hilbert was visibly delighted with Colt's anniversary flowers. "They're lovely. Just let me take them out to my van. I have a little something for you, too."

Colt's heart sank when she returned with a wheelchair. "Paula told you I fell?"

"You fell? Gracious, young man. Why didn't you say so? Are you injured? Let's have a look."

A "look" became a "prod" until at length, Mrs. Hilbert concluded that Colt needed to do the very thing he had hoped to avoid. The wheelchair that she had brought to give him greater independence and mobility proved indispensable in avoiding an ambulance ride to the hospital. Mrs. Hilbert loaded him into her handicapped-accessible van instead and parked her flowers in his lap to prevent them from toppling over en route.

Joy had cleared away dinner and washed up the dishes in Paula's absence. Paula went in to tell her good-night, and found her at her computer, writing.

"Homework?" she asked.

"No. I'm working on my story, the one Shelby gave me."

"I see." Paula was careful to keep her voice neutral.

"Dad said wrap it up."

"I don't think that's what he meant."

"I know what he meant. Shelby's getting married in May, so that isn't a lot of time to finish it."

"A gift bag and a card would be a lot simpler," said Paula.

"Cute, Mom. You're almost as clever as Dad. Now if you don't mind, I have a lot of work to do."

"Then you *are* returning it?"

"I guess. We wouldn't want to disappoint Dad, now would we?" Joy dropped her head back, and rolled her blue eyes.

Gratified that Colt had turned her thinking around, Paula celebrated a partial victory. She kissed her finger and pressed it to her little drama queen's fresh mouth. "Good night, sweetheart."

Pleasantly tired, Paula enjoyed a leisurely bath, then curled up with the novel she'd attempted to read that afternoon.

But once she turned the lights out, her thoughts flew to Colt. As dear as the moments they had spent together were, she wanted and needed to hear that he loved her. Or was her view self-centered?

Joy's relationship with Colt blossomed day to day, even in correction. Maybe she *could* accept reconciliation on such terms. For Joy's sake. Call it a renewed effort to keep the initial covenant they had made.

But what of hurt and wounded pride? It had proved a powerful dividing force in the past. Jealousy, too. In the depths of her heart, Paula had always feared there had been another woman in Colt's life. That fear played a part in the negative feelings she had concerning Monique. Paula shoved her suspicions aside. But they kept popping up again.

As always, Paula circled back to the same haunting question: Why had he walked away, convinced he couldn't live with her?

Ask him.

Paula wasn't the author of that suggestion. Needing rest, she shelved the often-pondered *why*. Curling her arm beneath her, she nestled her fist to her chin and slept.

Chapter Thirteen

The emergency room doctor took some X rays and examined Colt so thoroughly, even Mrs. Hilbert was satisfied that there was no need to admit him to the hospital.

It was after midnight when they finally arrived back at the lodge, too late to phone Paula. Mrs. Hilbert helped Colt to bed and fetched his laptop for him before letting herself out.

With each day that had passed, Colt's hopes of hearing from Monique had grown a little dimmer. Therefore, he was thunderstruck to find her e-mail waiting.

Dear Jig-Saw,
I'm sorry you got hurt, but my intentions were noble. Friends help friends, and I

thought you were my friend. Once I learned what had happened, I came to the hospital to see you, but you were sleeping. Things got a little hairy, and with Simon on the rampage, it was too risky to wait around. My friend Patrick says nothing's impossible with God, and that I should trust Him. I'm trying, but it isn't easy after living by my own wits all this time. I forgive you for deceiving me, and wish you a speedy recovery.
Monique.

Despite the lateness of the hour, Colt phoned Walt with the news. On Walt's advice, he called police headquarters and spoke with Detective Browning.

In so doing, Colt learned that Lefty Banks had signed a confession stating he was driving the car that struck Colt. Banks also claimed that he and his partner Hunter Cates had gone to Monique's house with orders from Simon Burwell to retrieve the incriminating postcard, and if possible, collect Monique as well. They now had an arrest warrant for Simon Burwell.

"I notified the Wyoming authorities right away. They are reopening their files on Myrtle Byron's death and are very anxious to talk with Monique. Give her my number. Wherever she is, we'll pick her up. Full police protection," he emphasized.

Colt drafted an e-mail to that effect and re-read Monique's missive. Patrick Delaney's name stuck out like a sore thumb. All at once, something Paula said in connection to Delaney and Shelby's intended honeymoon destination leaped to the foreground. Wildwood! It was such a long shot, Colt decided to sleep on it.

The possibility, though slim, still seemed feasible in the morning. Colt knew that he'd be pursuing it at his own peril where his future with Paula was concerned—Monique's name continued to be a hot button with her. Hearing water running next door, he picked up the phone and dialed Paula's number.

"Good morning! I thought I heard you stirring over there."

"Yes. Joy's going to walk to the church garden with me this morning if you'd like to come along," she invited. "Or are you up to it, after your fall?"

"I'm up to it. But I'm running a little behind, so I think I'll pass."

"If you called to talk to Joy, she's in the shower. I'll have her call you back," offered Paula.

"Or we could just chat until she's free," said Colt.

"Fine with me," Paula said. "What do you want to talk about?"

"Anything. Pick a subject. Any subject."

Paula's morning voice conveyed a smile. "I haven't had my coffee yet. How about I let you pick?" she accommodated him nicely.

"Very well, then. Tell me about Wildwood."

"Outside Liberty Flats? *That* Wildwood?"

"Yes."

"It's a nice place with a lovely view. Part farm, part timber, part campground. Why do you ask?" said Paula.

"Filler conversation, remember."

"Right." Paula chuckled.

"So tell me, who operates the place?" asked Colt.

"Trace and Thomasina Austin. They cater to church groups and at-risk children, though not to the exclusion of the general public. There are private cabins, a bed-and-breakfast, and dorm-style cabins for church camps,'' Paula said.

''If I were to make reservations, how far in advance would I have to do so?'' Colt circumvented all mention of Monique.

''It's off-season. I doubt very much that you'd need reservations.''

''That's good to know. In the event of a second honeymoon, for instance.'' He couldn't resist trying the idea out on her.

''Anyone I know?'' she countered.

He chuckled. ''You.''

''I'll pass for now. But I would agree to pick up where we left off last evening,'' she said.

''Talking?''

''Yes, *talking*,'' she replied with emphasis. ''What did you think?''

''I'd rather tell you in person,'' he said. ''Will you have breakfast with me?''

''If you don't mind waiting a bit,'' said Paula.

''That's fine. Bring Joy with you.'' Colt named a restaurant that boasted round-the-clock down-home cooking and bluegrass music. ''I'll have Mrs. Hilbert drop me by.''

''She's there now?''

"No. But I expect her any time. I'll call you if I'm running late. Oh, by the way, I have some good news. The police have the hit-and-run driver in custody."

Paula gave a glad cry of relief. "Why didn't you say so?"

"I hated to start the morning off on that note," claimed Colt.

"But they've got the right guy?"

"He signed a confession." Briefly, Colt filled her in on what Detective Browning had related to him by phone.

"What about the hospital scare? With Joy, I mean. Is Banks the one?" asked Paula.

"I'm afraid not. He was in court at the time." Colt related what he had learned from Walt.

"Who, then?" asked Paula.

"I don't know. Simon Burwell *could* have sent another thug or gone to the hospital himself, I guess," said Colt, though privately he couldn't feature Burwell involving himself in such foolhardy melodramatics as Joy described.

"To cover the tracks of those he hired," said Paula. "That could get to be an endless job. The more men he involves in his dirty work, the higher the odds someone's going to snitch on him.''

''Exactly. I'm still working through that one.'' Colt kept his growing doubts concerning Joy's story to himself.

A small silence followed. When Paula spoke, it was to say, ''I'd very much like to go home. Do you think it's safe?''

''Might be a good idea to wait until Burwell is in custody first.''

''Do they know where he is?''

''No.'' Colt again decided against bringing up Monique's name, and Browning's hope that she could provide information concerning her ex-husband's whereabouts.

But in her next breath, Paula pursued a similar thread, asking, ''Has Walt heard from that fellow Delaney?''

''Yes, as a matter of fact, Delaney did return his call to say he and Monique had shared a seat on the church bus coming home from the retreat.'' Colt related what Walt had told him.

''So she was telling the truth about the retreat!'' said Paula. ''Go figure.''

''Caught me by surprise, too,'' admitted Colt.

"Does Delaney know where she is now?"

"He says he hasn't seen her since the retreat," said Colt.

"Would he lie to protect her?" asked Paula.

"I have no idea," said Colt.

"Are they an item?" she asked.

"Just friends, I think. Why?"

"I just wondered."

Colt feared she might view it presumptuous of him, should he once again underscore the fact that his interest in Monique was purely business. He was spared a response, because Paula spoke into his hesitation, saying, "Joy's out of the shower now. Hold on, I'll call her to the phone."

Colt tested the waters to see if Joy was still feeling bruised over his advice concerning Shelby's book. Apparently her annoyance had dissipated in the night. She wanted to know if he was able to take the tram ride up the mountainside. Or would that be too strenuous for him on his crutches?

Mrs. Hilbert arrived to kick-start Colt's day just as he got off the phone. It took her awhile to check his healing wounds and make him presentable. She agreed to drop him by the restaurant.

Colt thanked her and didn't object when she suggested he use the wheelchair. "I need to make one last call first, if you'll excuse me."

Mrs. Hilbert tactfully withdrew, giving Colt the privacy he needed in able to be forthright in sharing his hunch with Detective Browning.

"Wildwood? Never heard of it," responded Detective Browning.

"Delaney has. He once planned to honeymoon there."

"Cue me on this Delaney," said Browning.

"He's a corporate attorney. People seem to think well of him. He volunteers at the Can-Do Mission, which is where he met Monique. He's tried to help her back on her feet, finding her affordable housing, that sort of thing. He even lined her up with a computer so she could work on another book. It's possible he mentioned Wildwood to her. Maybe in passing, or—"

"You think he's tucked her away there?" Browning was quick to the point.

"It's a long shot," said Colt. "But there'd be no harm in checking."

Browning warned Colt not to tell anyone that

he had heard from Monique, or mention his notion about Wildwood.

"Then you're going to follow through?"

"You bet," said Browning.

If Monique proved to be in Wildwood, the whole thing could come down quickly. *Profile Magazine* could be first with the in-depth story. To that end, Colt said, "Call and let me know what you learn. If this pans out, I'd like to cover it ahead of the pack."

"I understand. By the way, I've hit a lot of dead ends, looking for whoever it was who threatened your daughter. I'm stumped on motivation, too," added Browning.

It jarred Colt to hear his own doubts echoed by a professional. He said nothing.

"Is your girl capable of making up a story like that?" pressed Browning.

Torn over the possibility and reluctant to discuss it, particularly with the police, Colt said, "You're asking the wrong person."

"What's her mother say about it?"

"It hasn't come up," said Colt.

"It's time it did. Take it up with Mrs. Blake," said Browning.

And say what? wondered Colt. *By the way,*

*babe, Detective Browning has some serious
doubts about Joy's truthfulness.*

Colt braced himself for fireworks and tried
Paula on the phone. There was no answer. Was
she out walking? Or at the restaurant, waiting?
Running out of time, Colt rolled himself out to
the parking lot. The lift on Mrs. Hilbert's van
expedited matters. She anchored his wheelchair
securely, and was about to pull away when
Colt's cell phone chirped.

"Browning here. Thanks for the hot tip."

Startled, Colt motioned for Mrs. Hilbert to
wait. "That didn't take long," he said to
Browning.

"Accomplished it by phone."

"And?"

"Bingo!" said Browning.

"Does she know you're coming?" Colt followed the detective's cautious suit and didn't
mention Monique's name.

"No. I don't want to spook her. How's your
rapport with her?"

"Not bad," said Colt. "I'd be willing to tag
along and break the ice for you."

"I was hoping you'd say that. How soon can

you catch a flight back to the city?'' asked Browning.

"I'll get right on it."

"Good. We'll work on the details once you get here."

At Colt's request, Mrs. Hilbert went inside and fetched his laptop and his crutches while he checked with the airlines. There was a flight to Chicago scheduled to leave just before noon. Unwilling to wait that long, Colt phoned a charter service. As luck would have it, he was able to make arrangements to fly out immediately.

En route to the airport, Colt tried to reach Paula to cancel their breakfast date. But she didn't answer her cell phone, nor did she answer his page at the restaurant. At a loss, he penned a note which Mrs. Hilbert agreed to deliver to the lodge.

"You're a jewel, Mrs. Hilbert," he said, and tipped her generously for her trouble.

Chapter Fourteen

Paula changed into a sleeveless jungle print dress. Slim fitting through the bodice, it fell in light folds to a silken whisper a few inches above her ankles. She accessorized with gold sandals and wood-carved elephant jewelry.

"It's a nice dress. You look great, Mom." Joy trekked out the door behind her and into the lush Smoky Mountain morning. "A little upscale for a hike. But it's perfect for a romantic down-home, hoedown breakfast. Maybe we can drop by that little wedding chapel afterward. I'll be your flower girl."

"We're not having this conversation," said Paula.

Joy cocked her head in that voice-of-reason mode of hers and forestalled Paula's objections with an uplifted hand. "But if we were, I'd want you to know that I *know* there's no law says you *have* to repeat your vows before you try again. But what would be the harm in giving it a fresh face? You know, the way you would a peeling sign?"

Joy tramped along at Paula's side to the garden and back, cheerfully flinging Cupid arrows.

"Be thinking what you want for breakfast." Paula sought valiantly to sidetrack her.

"Cold cereal at my computer."

"You're not eating with us?" said Paula, surprised.

"I have to get my schoolwork done so we can take the tram up the mountain this afternoon. You can sit in the middle. That way, Dad can get his arm around you, should you get claustrophobic."

"On an open-air tram? I don't think that will be a problem," said Paula dryly.

"You can always pretend." Joy batted her lashes. "Work with me, Mom. Work with me."

A cozy breakfast, minus the matchmaker, was sounding more appealing all the time. Once back to the lodge, Paula grabbed her keys, blew Joy a kiss and locked up on her way out.

Paula arrived a few minutes early, took a table in full view of the door and sipped coffee while she waited.

Three refills later, she got concerned and tried to reach Colt by phone. He didn't answer at the lodge. Nor could she reach him on his cell phone. Paula dialed Joy, hoping she might shed some light. But Joy didn't answer, either.

Paula left her name and a message with the restaurant hostess, in the event Colt showed up. Back at the lodge, she found Joy slouched before her computer, hands idle in her lap.

"I tried to call you. Didn't you hear the phone?"

Joy mumbled something. Paula couldn't make heads or tails of it. "I waited an hour at the restaurant. Your dad never showed up."

"He went home," said Joy, eyes fixed on the screen.

"He's next door, then?"

"Home, home. It's all in the note."

"What note?" asked Paula, her tone as sharp as Joy's was dull.

"It was taped to the door."

Braced, Paula retraced her steps. She found a piece of fresh tape, but no note. She trekked back to Joy's room with growing impatience.

"There is no note. Turn around here, and talk to me."

With marked reluctance, Joy stretched out her left arm and opened her fist. Shredded paper fell to the floor.

"You tore up his note?" Paula's disbelief rang shrill in the pin drop silence. "Joy! What on earth is wrong with you?"

Joy swiveled and tipped her tearstained face. "He left us, Mom! He did it again. And this time, he knew all about me!"

Paula's heart plummeted as the dam burst on Joy's pent-up anguish. It was as if a vacuum had sucked all the air from her lungs. *This couldn't be happening. Not again!*

"He's mean, mean, mean! I don't ever want to see him again. Not ever!"

Joy flung herself at Paula. Twin sledgehammers lashing at her temples, Paula wrapped her child, her whole world, in her embrace and rocked her, murmuring inane reassurances.

Eventually, Joy's stormy tempest subsided. She withdrew to blow her nose and wash her

face, giving Paula a much needed moment of
privacy. Carefully, she gathered up the pieces
of the note and took sanctuary in her own room.
With trembling hands, she pieced the torn
scraps until the note came together:

> Dear Paula,
> Urgent business. Returned to Chicago. De-
> tective Browning's investigation sheds
> doubt on Joy's story. What do you think?
> Is she in the habit of lying? I'll be in touch.
>
> > Love,
> > Colt

Love. The word blurred before Paula's eyes.
''Love always protects, always trusts, always
hopes, always perseveres.'' *So where are you,
Colt?*

Chicago. Urgent business. Childhood lyrics
taunted, *Loves me. Loves me not.* A wave of
raw emotion propelled Paula from the present
to the torn shore of that long-ago abandonment.
But she picked herself up and wiped her eyes
and scanned once more the pieced note.

This time, she needn't wonder where he was
or why he'd gone. He had a lead on his story,

she'd bet her life on it. He was tracking down Monique. Even a child could read between the thin blue lines of his patched note. *Her* child, opening the door, watching her from eyes too large for her face.

Paula knew all too well the wounding that had driven Joy to destroying Colt's note. Maternal instinct prodded her past the quicksand of self-pity and the illusion that love in all its facets was a sham. She emptied her lungs of trapped air, dried her eyes and came to a decision.

"Get your things together, Joy. We're going home."

"Home?" cried Joy. "But isn't that the first place he'll look?"

"You're a big girl. You don't have to see your father if you don't want to," said Paula.

"Not Dad! The guy at the hospital," screeched Joy. "Or don't *you* believe me, either?"

Indeed, there was a seed of doubt where there had been none before. Paula gave no thought to watering it. "Of course I believe you," she said firmly. "But we can't let fear rule our lives.

We'll take precautions. We can stay with Jake and Gram until we've worked through this."

"Mom! Would you listen to yourself? What's changed? Nothing! Nothing's changed!" Fingers splayed, Joy's skinny arms waved like saplings in a wind storm.

Paula rubbed her throbbing head in an effort to clear the debris. At length she said, "Perhaps I should check with Detective Browning first."

"What for? He's the one who made Dad think I'm a liar!"

"Walt Snyder, then," amended Paula. He was kind and genuine and protective. He was also Colt's boss and friend. Vetoing that idea as quickly as it surfaced, Paula caught Joy's hand in hers and prayed for guidance.

The tumult in her inner being quieted. Trusting in His protection, she booked a flight back to Chicago.

The plane landed in Chicago in weather as dreary as the gray walls of her weary heart. They took a cab to Shelby's apartment building under leaden skies and retrieved her car. It was a long rainy ride home.

Paula parked her car in the steel building behind Gram's house. The building housed Jackson Signs, her office and the room where she shaped neon for signs. She and Joy trekked in and caught Gram and Jake by surprise.

It was good to be home. But the explanations were almost as wearying as the experience itself. Paula was relieved to tumble into the four-poster feather bed where she had slept in the years following her parents' death and her marriage to Colt.

Morning came, sunrise obscured by a blanket of fog. Paula dressed in black jeans and a powder-blue T-shirt emblazoned with the Jackson Sign Company logo. She fussed her hair into place, and swathed a little color and a lipsticked mouth on the drawn face in the mirror. She was making breakfast when her sister Wendy arrived.

Jake, Joy and Gram joined them at the table. Paula was careful to remain impersonal concerning Colt as she brought them up to date over bacon and eggs and biscuits. Afterward, Wendy drove Gram to adult daycare, freeing Paula to take Joy to school before work. She talked to the principal briefly, revealing no more than necessary, but enough to raise the level of awareness and security concerning Joy's safety.

Back at the sign shop, she listened as Jake brought her up to speed concerning work orders. One for Wildwood was on top of the pile. Paula's friend, Annie Penn, who worked for the Austins, had phoned twice to complain the neon welcome sign was on the blink.

Paula donned a company windbreaker to ward off the damp fog. Joy had napped beneath her nearly completed quilt on the way home. It was still in the back seat. Paula folded it to one side and put her toolbox on the floor.

Knowing Annie would have a pot of coffee brewing, she stopped for sweets at Newt's Market. Earl Newton rang her up at the front register.

"Morning, Paula. Did you get a load of that?" With a jerk of his white head, Newton indicated a sleek late-model limousine parked in the loading zone beyond his wide front window.

Paula looked to see two men in dark suits

and hats and dark glasses climb out of the front seat.

"Feds, I'll wager," drawled old Newt. "Guess they can't read."

Paula eyeballed the showy car parked right next to Newt's freshly painted No Parking sign. "Give them a ticket, Newt."

Newt chortled and gave her her change. Paula pulled up her parka hood to keep her hair from going flat in the weather and let herself out.

The two men passed her on the sidewalk. Neither acknowledged her. Through the tinted windows, Paula saw a third man in the back seat. He was reading the newspaper and appeared not to notice her passing.

Paula explained away an uneasy stir as too much fog and imagination. She rounded the corner to the side street where she had left her car and climbed in. The road to Wildwood ran between fields and woodlands. It wasn't uncommon to spot deer grazing in the grassy ditches early in the morning.

Paula snapped on her headlights and made the short trip without incident. A long lane led to the farmhouse that served as a bed-and-breakfast and reception office. Paula made the turn, then braked in surprise. Dead ahead a closed gate blocked the lane.

She drummed her fingers on the steering wheel and weighed her options. Unlock the gate? Or should she backtrack to the gravel road and take the back lane?

Seeing no point in getting out in the damp, Paula shifted into reverse. She hit the gas and looked back just as an oncoming car emerged from the fog. Had it been passing on the road, she could have stopped in time. But it was turning in.

Paula couldn't brake quickly enough. The bumper to bumper collision sent her head into the steering wheel. Stars danced in the fog. She shifted into park and blinked them away. And blinked again. But try as she might, Paula couldn't erase the picture of Colt on crutches, jerking at her car door.

Chapter Fifteen

"Paula! Are you all right? Unlock your door!" Colt's voice penetrated Paula's shell-shocked ears.

It was surreal, dreamlike. Unfolding as if in slow motion. As Paula peered through the glass, a second man approached her window. Something about him was familiar, though displaced. In her punchy state, it took Paula a moment.

Fighting the cobwebs, she found the button, lowered the window and squinted. "Detective Browning?"

The detective tipped his hat. "Good morning, Mrs. Blake."

"It *is* you."

"Yes, ma'am. Do you need medical assistance, Mrs. Blake?"

"N-no, I don't think so," stammered Paula.

"Are you sure?" Colt shouldered in next to the detective. The color was gone from his face. His alarm was tangible. She could feel it in his fingertips as he reached in and tipped her chin.

"You've bumped your head."

His touch gave rise to disturbing sensations. Paula put the car in park, turned off the key and checked her forehead in the mirror. "It's just a scratch. What about you?"

"You barely tapped us. We're all fine." Colt's gaze followed as she fingered the tender spot on her forehead. "You're getting some swelling there. How's your vision?"

Paula watched Detective Browning circling behind her car to check for damage. He made a crisp image in the wispy fog. "I can see just fine."

Colt produced a key chain from his pocket, switched on the small flashlight hanging from it, and shone it in her eyes. "Can you follow the light?"

It was less disconcerting to do his bidding

than to admit it was his presence, not the bump, that stunned her. *What was he doing here?*

The sleeve of Colt's raincoat rustled as he switched off the light and returned the keys to his pocket. Detective Browning circled back to report minor dents. Colt took him aside. Paula's ears had stopped roaring. She listened as he lowered his voice.

"You gentlemen go on ahead without me. I'll see she gets back to town safely."

"You dally too long, and you'll miss your scoop," warned the officer.

"I don't want her on the road alone," said Colt.

"Very well, then," said Detective Browning.

Both men stepped back to Paula's open window.

"You want to slide over and I'll drive?" Colt asked Paula as Detective Browning reached to open the door.

"I can't go yet," protested Paula. "I have a service order. I drove out here to pick up a sign."

"I'm sorry, but this isn't a good time. The proprietors are gone, and the desk clerk has the day off," said Colt.

"Is that right, Detective Browning?" asked Paula.

"Yes, ma'am. If you're ready to go, Mr. Blake will accompany you back to town."

"Very well, then. But I'm going to drive," said Paula.

The detective shot Colt a wordless glance, then circled Paula's car and tucked the crutches in back with her tools. Colt folded himself into the passenger's seat. Detective Browning clapped him on the shoulder, closed the car door and strode toward the gate.

"You need to back up and let them through," Colt prompted as the officer swung it open.

Paula did as he said. The car pulled through, picked up Detective Browning and continued up the lane. Accident jitters gave way to a deeper concern. She shot Colt an anxious glance. "Is somebody hurt?"

"Everybody's fine. So far," he added. "Let's head back to town."

"Why? What's going on? Tell me, Colt!"

"Browning's baited a trap for Burwell. You can't say anything to anyone. Not a word."

His steely calm only heightened her alarm. "Simon Burwell's here?"

"Not yet. But he will be, if everything works according to plan."

"But why?"

"He's coming for the postcard. Monique's waiting in the honeymoon cabin to exchange it and her silence for a king's ransom," Colt told her.

Monique. She'd been right, then. He'd left them for her. Paula shifted into gear by rote and eased her foot onto the accelerator.

"Monique's been hiding out here for the past week and a half. It was your linking Patrick Delaney to this place that led to our finding her," Colt continued.

"A phone call determined that a woman answering to Monique's description was indeed here at Wildwood. Detective Browning thought I might prove useful. So I flew back to Chicago, and came down. You get my note?"

Paula nodded, the lines between past and present as blurred as the haze that swallowed the road ahead and behind her.

"I rode down with Browning and broke the ice with Monique. She quickly warmed up to the idea of phoning Burwell and offering to sell him the incriminating postcard.'' Colt resumed his account.

''She knew where to reach him?'' Paula stirred herself to ask.

''No. Browning had her leave a number on his answering machine. Sure enough, Burwell called back and agreed to her terms.''

''She's gutsy, I'll give her that,'' said Paula grudgingly.

''Who, Monique?'' Colt nodded. ''She knows the stakes are high. But Browning has had protective forces in place since yesterday when she made the call.

''How about you?'' continued Colt. ''I tried all day and half the night to call you. Where've you been?''

''At Gram Kate's,'' said Paula. ''Why?''

''I was worried about you,'' he said. ''We drove by your grandmother's house last night, but I didn't see your car.''

''I parked it in the sign shop.'' Paula reduced her speed to accommodate decreasing visibility. ''Who's *we?*''

''I was with Detective Browning. Who'd you think?''

Paula's hackles rose that he had the audacity to ask. "You stand me up and take off to rescue Monique. What am I supposed to think?"

"You're not jealous, are you?"

"I'm going to pretend I didn't hear that," she countered.

"Look. I'm sorry. Time got tight. I tried your cell phone, but I couldn't reach you. Is your battery down again?"

"I don't know. Does it matter?"

Colt scratched his head. "There you go again. Every time Monique's name comes up, you get that attitude."

"And what would you have my attitude to be?" she countered.

"I don't know. It seems out of character for you, that's all." He pinched his mouth a moment, then added, "I'll say it again, just for the record—I've got a story to write. That's where my interest in Monique starts and ends."

A sudden patch of pea soup fog spared Paula the obligatory reply. She sat forward and rubbed from the windshield the steam of their heated debate. Failing at that, she lowered her window. The car slowed to a crawl.

"You'll get rear-ended if you're not careful. Pick it up a little," warned Colt.

"I'm trying." Paula gave it more gas. The car bucked. "Something's wrong. Feel that?"

"Check your gas gauge," said Colt.

The needle was in the red. "Oh, brother! Not again," she muttered.

"Pull over. You don't want to stall in the middle of the road."

"I don't want to stall at all!"

"Then maybe you should try to remember to put gas in the tank," Colt suggested mildly.

"And maybe you should try to remember where your priorities lie. And I'm not talking about me!" Paula retorted.

She turned on her hazard lights and prayed Jake hadn't left the sign shop yet. A premature request, as it turned out. The battery was indeed down on her cell phone. She reached for the door.

Colt's hand shot out to stop her. "You're not going to walk, are you?"

"It's no more than a mile to town," reasoned Paula.

"It's too dense out there. Just sit tight. We

can kill time sorting out my priorities, if you like.''

''They're pretty clear. You left *us* to look for *Monique*,'' said Paula.

''The risk had passed,'' he reasoned. ''Burwell's hired thugs were both locked up.''

''What about the guy who threatened Joy?''

''Detective Browning expressed reasonable doubts,'' said Colt.

''He's wrong,'' said Paula.

''I hope you're right. But think back, Paula,'' Colt reasoned with her. ''When I first mentioned Walt's offer to tuck us away until Burwell and his thugs were under lock and key, you refused.''

''That was before Joy was threatened,'' protested Paula.

''My point exactly. The question is, did she manipulate you into changing your mind?''

''By saying she'd been accosted and threatened? I can't believe you'd suspect your own daughter of such a thing.''

''I don't know my own daughter,'' replied Colt.

''I do. She's devastated that you believe she's lying,'' cried Paula.

''I don't know what to believe. That's why I asked for your opinion.''

''In writing. Where she found it.'' Paula drove her point home.

''I didn't think about that.''

He looked so stricken, Paula said quickly, ''I'm sorry, Colt. But it's the truth.''

Colt dragged his hand over his face. Abruptly, he reached into his coat pocket, withdrew his cell phone, and slid it across the seat to her.

He could have spared them both, had he done so in the first place. Paula averted her eyes, and dialed the sign shop. Jake was helping the men load a sign. But he agreed to bring her a can of gas just as soon as he was free.

A slow drizzle picked holes in the fog as they waited. Paula hugged the door on the driver's side. She was about to drown in the silence when twin lights penetrated the damp horizon. Reprieve in shouting distance, she reached for the door. But it wasn't Jake's truck, rather, a sleek black late-model sedan emerging from the mists.

Startled, she blurted, ''Them, again!''

Colt stirred to attention. ''Locals?''

"No, strangers. I saw them in town earlier. They stuck out like sore thumbs in their suits and dark glasses."

"Dark glasses? In this fog?" Shifting, Colt studied the car as it passed. His jaw hardened. He retrieved his cell phone and was punching numbers when twin taillights broke through the thinning mists.

Paula jerked at Colt's arm. "Look! They're backing up."

"It's Burwell. If he sees me, he'll slither back under his rock," rasped Colt.

"He knows you?" cried Paula.

Colt conceded as much with a curt nod.

"Duck down in the seat," Paula said, ducking.

"It's a little late for that. We've already got their attention. Why else would they back up?"

He tapped an impatient hand, waiting for Browning to answer his phone. "Come on, come on, pick it up."

His urgency sparked a desperate idea in Paula.

"Ballgame's on. Triple header. One mile from town. Batter's out of the box. Keep your ears on." Colt gave Browning a coded thumbs-up, even as Paula flung the quilt over his shoulders and pulled the folds up around his face.

"Are you kidding?" he scoffed.

"Just try!" Paula caught his hands to keep him from throwing off the quilt. "Pretend you're sedated. Stare straight ahead. Don't say a word!"

She pulled up her parka hood and sprang from the car. "Hey!" yelped Colt.

Paula glanced back and caught such a look of horror on his face, she dared not look again. The wind blew her hood back and unraveled her mane of red hair. Fear compressed her lungs. But with a fierce prayer, she bounced on her toes and waved her arms in the autumn drizzle.

The sedan crawled along in reverse, and braked even with her. A shaded back window came down. Simon Burwell took off his dark glasses, and stared. Paula approached his car window, feigning relief.

"Bless you for coming back! I've run out of gas. I've got a patient with me. He's only been out of the ward a few days." Paula flung an arm to indicate the quilt-shrouded shape in the passenger's seat. She tapped her temple. "He's cold and scared and about to break down, and if he does, I'm not sure I can handle him. Do you have a phone I could use?''

The man's shaded eyes flicked over her dismissively. He motioned to the driver, and sat back in the seat. The car rolled ahead, the tires sucking at the wet pavement.

''How about sending some help, then? Please! Where are you going? You could at least make a call. Is that so much to ask?''

Arms akimbo, Paula threw herself into a foot-stamping picture of disgust. She dared not turn back until the car disappeared over the rise. Legs losing their starch, Paula fled back to her car. She clamored in, dripping rain. ''He thought I was her. Didn't he? *That's* why he came back!'' she bleated.

Colt's lack of color was all that gave him away. He gripped her arms with trembling hands and pulled her across the seat, muttering, ''You and your Miss Clairol. Shed your jacket, you're dripping wet.''

Keeping one arm around her, Colt hit redial on his phone, and barked another coded message to Browning.

Teeth chattering, shaking uncontrollably,

Paula stammered, "J-just like me. Falling apart when it's all over."

"You saved the day," said Colt. "Get the blood flowing now, and pray Browning drops the net without incident."

Bolstered by his praise, his lethal calm, and most of all, his pragmatism, Paula melted unprotestingly against him, enjoying a comforting hug within the folds of Joy's quilt.

"You should be there. You're going to miss your scoop." Paula echoed Browning's words with new insight.

"Do you hear me complaining?" said Colt.

"Maybe you should be."

Colt smiled and smoothed her damp hair. "That was good acting, babe. You want to explain to me again why I'm a thoroughly rotten father for thinking Joy might get creative in a similar fashion, should the stakes be high enough?"

Had the heat wave in her cheeks spread itself evenly, Paula could have thrown off the quilt. As it was, she murmured, "Let's not start that again."

"You're right. Let's not." He grazed the top of her hair with his lips. "Hot, isn't it?"

"Are you kidding? I'm freez..." Paula stopped short, cued by his slow and steady smile. Warmth came in undulating waves. Rainwater trailed from her hair down her neck. "It's not the heat, it's this awful humidity," she amended.

He kissed a damp rivulet from her ear and laughed. The sound of it rustled like corn shucks stirred by a soft breeze. His lips moved over her mouth, then took an intermission to say, "Are you willing to try again?"

"And make Joy's dream come true?"

"Is it your dream? That's what I'm asking," pressed Colt.

"That depends on you," said Paula. "If you could have anything in the world, what would it be?"

"A second chance," he said simply.

Paula's eyes filled. "Me, too."

Colt's kisses drew her in and covered her over, shutting out the world.

Chapter Sixteen

Paula slipped over to the driver's side and jumped out of the car as a company sign truck pulled into view. Paula hadn't mentioned Colt, so Jake's surprise was to be expected. Paula explained as best she could while Jake poured the gas in the tank and got the car running again.

Heaping blessings on Jake, Paula turned the Crown Vic around and drove Colt back to Wildwood. They arrived in time for him to collect his camera from Detective Browning's car and snap some shots of Burwell as he was helped into the back seat of a squad car.

Leaving Colt to his story, Paula angled to-

ward the closed-in porch which served as Wildwood's greeting center.

A lithe poncho-and-jean-clad figure came
down the stone path toward her. Something in
the face was familiar. The eyes! It was the halo
of red hair that confused Paula momentarily.
Then suddenly, it all fell into place.

"Monique?" she said to be sure.

The woman responded with a wordless flick
of wary eyes and thick lashes. "Do I know
you?" she asked, in the throaty tenor voice
Paula recalled so clearly.

"No. I'm Colt's wife. We bumped into one
another at the hospital in Chicago," said Paula.

"We did? Oh, you! You were coming off the
elevator. Of course," said Monique.

"As you were stepping in, dressed to de-
ceive," countered Paula. "It was a clever disguise. Fooled me. My daughter, too. Except she
mistook you for a thug."

A dark stain crept over Monique's face. She
looked beyond Paula. "I needed to see for myself that you were okay, Colt."

Paula turned to see Colt standing behind her.
She retreated a step and slipped an arm around

him. Tipping her face, she said, "Burwell wasn't behind it. It was her."

"I heard," said Colt, as Paula indicated Monique. "What on earth were you thinking?" he demanded of Monique.

"I'm trying to explain," Monique said defensively. "I realized at a glance that the girl was your daughter. But what I needed to say couldn't be said to a child. And you were asleep, Colt. So I asked her where you were, Mrs. Blake. And for some reason, she went to pieces on me."

"After you threatened her!" exclaimed Paula.

"I didn't threaten her," said Monique.

"Oh? I suppose you didn't shake her, either," said Paula, bristling.

"I may have caught her shoulder. But I was trying to calm her."

"By telling her it was a bad day to die?" said Paula, incredulous.

"I didn't mean *her*. I meant me. And I would have, too, if Simon had had his way." Looking out to the yard, Monique indicated the squad car that was now pulling away with Simon Burwell inside.

Abruptly, Paula's anger dissipated. While Monique's account didn't parallel Joy's, it was close enough. She was willing to give her the benefit of the doubt, and forgive her for scaring Joy. Accepting that Joy's tempest and all the angst since had been born of overactive imagination and miscommunication, Paula rubbed her throbbing head, and shot Colt a wary glance.

"So we were both right," he said gently.

In a manner of speaking. Paula's conscience nudged. "I owe you an apology," she murmured.

"Then you believe me?" said Monique.

Paula tipped her face. But before she could clarify to whom she was apologizing, Colt hugged her to his side. "We'll talk later. I have work to do."

"Me, too," said Paula.

Excusing herself, she went to see about the Welcome sign. At length, Colt and Monique came into the office to continue their interview. Watching Colt as she puttered with the sign, Paula took pride in his professional demeanor and rebuked her former suspicions. It was a quiet realization, but pivotal. His love was a love she could trust.

Unable to fix the sign on the job site, Paula carried it out to the car, then returned for her tools. She spoke briefly with Colt.

"It looks as if it will be a while. But I'll catch a ride and stop by later to sort things out with Joy," said Colt.

Paula worked in the shop all day, stopping only to collect Joy from school. She hadn't wanted her to walk home, jumping at shadows that weren't there. But it was almost quitting time when Colt dropped by the sign shop.

"Joy's around here somewhere," said Paula, coming to her feet. "I told her all about the police catching Mr. Burwell, and all the rest, too."

"I know. She was skating on the driveway when Detective Browning dropped me off. We had a nice talk," said Colt.

Paula searched his face and found relief there. "She let you off the hook, did she?"

He arched a smile. "She's got her mother's forgiving heart."

"I was about to lock up. You want to come

home with me? I'll fix dinner, and we can talk.''

"I like the sound of that. But I'm afraid I'll have to take a rain check," he said.

"How come?" asked Paula.

"Walt's waiting for me to wrap this thing up so he can put this month's issue to bed. I've got notes at home I need to review.'' Circling behind her chair, Colt said, "You want a back rub before I go?''

"Better not. Joy's liable to pop in here and get the wrong idea,'' said Paula. "Or rather, the right one.''

Colt chuckled. "I'll take that chance.'' His hands fell to her shoulders.

"I'm not sure this is conducive to what I've been thinking about all afternoon,'' admitted Paula, pulse racing at his skilled touch.

"Oh? What's that?'' he asked, hands kneading.

"I'm cured of hurrying things and making mistakes. I want to take it easy this time. Show some patience and relish getting to know you.''

"A leisurely courtship. Is that what you're proposing?'' Colt leaned in and kissed her neck.

"That's right. I'd like to be private about it for a while, too, if we can."

"What about Joy?"

"It won't be easy to keep it from her. But once we tell her, our identity shifts," reasoned Paula. "We're Mom and Dad, then. I'd like to be…"

"Adam and Eve?" he offered helpfully.

Paula flushed, but lifted her eyes to his. "Before the fall. Just you and me and God. For a while anyway."

"How long is 'a while?'" asked Colt.

Paula had anticipated that question. "It takes nine months to bring a child into the world. Shouldn't we spend at least that much time building a strong home?"

"For Joy?"

"For us." Counting the months on her fingers, she said, "That'll take us into June. Then we'll let Joy in on our secret and welcome her into the nest."

"I didn't realize you were so fanciful," he said. "How do you plan to carry off this little intrigue?"

"We'll have to be discreet, and make the most of your visitation rights," said Paula.

He smiled faintly. "Who am I visiting?"

"Your family." Paula leaned back in the chair and collected the kiss waiting there on his lips. "Count on it."

Colt returned to Chicago that evening and did just that. Joy took the train up to spend Saturday and Sunday with him. As much as he enjoyed her company, he had vastly underestimated all that he had to learn concerning fatherhood. What he had viewed as a romantic whim on Paula's part, he now saw as fundamental to getting their new life off to a strong start.

He said as much in an e-mail to Paula. She responded with a sweet note. In closing, she wrote: "I'm praying God will help us put our marriage back together piece by piece that it might become a work of strength and endurance and lasting beauty. Like a lovely patchwork quilt."

Anticipation became the operative word from that moment forward. Colt sculpted his in-depth article on Simon Burwell so he could earn some free time to pursue the joys of his life. The day his issue hit the stands, he received an e-mail from Paula: "Dear Colt, Just finished the article. Wow! I'm impressed, and so proud of you. If not for your persistence, Simon Burwell would still be on the street. And who knows what would have become of Monique? Are you going to cover his trial?"

Colt not only covered it, he flew out to Wyoming and testified about the postcard, which played a key part in the prosecution's case. The trial was recessed over Christmas. Colt flew home to collect Joy, then on to his parents' home for a lovely old-fashioned white Christmas. It was Joy's first chance to meet them. C.J. and his sister's family arrived on Christmas Eve. It was a wonderful roller-coaster ride, an emotional experience which he shared with Paula by phone.

Two weeks later the jury came back with a guilty verdict on Burwell. Colt returned home and talked Paula into flying up to the city to celebrate. Afterward, Paula presented him with a gift box. Inside was a quilt top she had fashioned and machine quilted. It depicted a mountain stream, a canoe and a man with a type-writer on his lap.

"It's a quickie. A cut and iron," she said, making light of it when he thanked her. "That's you, typing Simon Burwell up the river."

He laughed and kissed her and stayed until dawn, anticipating the nights they would spend beneath that quilt. Looking down through the years he pictured them cradling round-faced babies with Jackson-blue eyes and yellow hair. Infant duplicates of Joy. Not to replace what they had missed, but rather to make the most of God's gift of a second chance. He anticipated noise and laughter and joy to fill Paula's child-hood home, which his attorney had so dis-creetly purchased on his behalf. Joy was in a dither, trying to solve the mystery of who owned the house and who would move in once the renovation was complete. Little did she know! Paula knew all about it. It was to be his gift to her at the culmination of their secret courtship. As such, it was important to him that it live up to her memories.

This too, he anticipated.

When Paula had suggested a secret courtship, she had had her doubts she could keep her feelings for Colt from Joy. However, their limited opportunities made a delicious secret of stolen glances and covert kisses. Moments when they were truly alone were nothing short of precious jewels.

Fall, winter and then spring thaw left a paper trail of cards and letters and e-mails. Freely, they shared their hearts concerning everything from past mistakes to future ambitions and secret fantasies.

And phone calls. They talked nearly every morning. Early, before Joy awakened. It was heaven to start the day that way. Often, they spoke in whispers of the home they would share as they divided their married life between Chicago and Liberty Flats. Paula was deeply touched by Colt's passion for restoring her childhood home.

But as Jake and Shelby's wedding date approached, Paula found herself growing impatient. She was happy for Jake. But at the same time, she dreaded that lonely "single in a double world" sensation she always got at family occasions. She shared as much with Colt in a late-night e-mail. He commiserated and unbeknownst to her, wheedled an invitation to the wedding through Joy.

When the day finally arrived, he put on his best suit and surprised Paula on the sunny shores of Lake Michigan where she and her family had gathered to witness Jake and Shelby exchanging vows. Dressed in a white suit with a yellow rose in her hair, Paula looked like a blushing bride herself. Surprise lighted her face. She smiled at him with happy tears as the pastor presented the newlyweds.

"What God has joined together, let no man put asunder. You may kiss your bride." The pastor winked at Jake.

But Colt seized the moment, too, and gathered Paula in his arms. All that anticipating made for good priming. Their kiss was so thorough, the men-folk jerked the knots from their ties and shifted their feet.

Paula's sisters went from wide-eyed to nervous smiles. Gram Kate tugged at her skirt with a sweet vacant look. But Joy was a one-girl picture show. She danced and hooted and hollered.

"I knew it! I knew it! You didn't fool me

for a second!'' Joy flung her arms around her parents and hugged so hard it hurt.

After her performance, Paula's announcement of a June renewal ceremony and reception was anticlimatic. But the second honeymoon surpassed expectations. As did the garden reception in their newly refurbished home in Liberty Flats.

*　*　*　*　*

Dear Reader,

Aren't the products available to today's quilters intriguing? Some time ago, I bought a bottle of Tack-It off a quilt-shop shelf—that's glue for a temporary bond. The bond remains tacky, enabling me to move about embellishments on varied textiles or even unfold a visual story that will stick to a quilt the way specially backed cutouts stick to flannel graph. That's tacky! That's good. That's very good.

But when applied to marriage, *temporary*, the relational equivalent of Tack-It, is a tragedy. *Temporary* loses its salt in an unsavory world. *Temporary* crumbles beneath the onslaught of personality clashes, prevailing whims, strong wills and difficult circumstances. The resulting broken hearts and vows, broken homes and broken children, are the scrap stash from which Paula and Colton's story is pieced. I relished taking their "trashed" marriage and turning it into a family treasure, for they epitomize all of us who are studying, hands on, the profound mystery of marriage and the unity spoken of in Ephesians 5:32. So be of good courage, dear reader, and pray with me a prayer that our world may be strengthened by durable, satisfying marriages and strong, healthy homes. God's faithfulness is an eternal adhesive and a tie that binds us to the Master Quilter. Praise and honor to His holy name.

Susan Kirby

LOVE COMES HOME

BY

TERRI REED

Rachel Maguire had always been sure of God's plan
for her—a career in medicine to improve hospital
conditions. That meant giving up the only man
she'd ever loved: Joshua Taylor. But twelve years
after she'd turned down his proposal, he was back
in her life, making her wonder: Did God's plan
for her include Josh and his young son?

Don't miss

LOVE COMES HOME

on sale June 2004

Available at your favorite retail outlet.

Take 2 inspirational love stories FREE!

PLUS get a FREE surprise gift!

Mail to Steeple Hill Reader Service

In U.S.
3010 Walden Ave.
P.O. Box 1867
Buffalo, NY 14240-1867

In Canada
P.O. Box 609
Fort Erie, Ontario
L2A 5X3

YES! Please send me 2 free Love Inspired® novels and my free surprise gift. After receiving them, if I don't wish to receive anymore, I can return the shipping statement marked cancel. If I don't cancel, I will receive 4 brand-new novels every month, before they're available in stores! Bill me at the low price of $3.99 each in the U.S. and $4.49 each in Canada, plus 25¢ shipping and handling and applicable sales tax, if any*. That's the complete price and a saving of over 10% off the cover prices—quite a bargain! I understand that accepting the books and gift places me under no obligation ever to buy any books. I can always return a shipment and cancel at any time. Even if I never buy another book from Steeple Hill, the 2 free books and the surprise gift are mine to keep forever.

113 IDN DU9F
313 IDN DU0G

Name	(PLEASE PRINT)	
Address	Apt. No.	
City	State/Prov.	Zip/Postal Code

A novel about the miracle of faith from award-winning author Sharon Gillenwater

Riding the stagecoach to Willow Grove, Texas, Camille Dupree hoped to leave behind her shocking secrets. Longing to reclaim her innocence and believe in the goodness of others, she was finally able to develop a reciprocal appreciation for her neighbors...especially the town's mayor, Tyler McKinnon, who saw more beauty and virtue in Camille than she'd ever seen in herself.

But the past was not far behind, and Camille soon found herself in need of the town's forgiveness...and Tyler's. Could she trust the man she loved to bend his principles and extend the pardon that would bless them both?

Steeple
Hill®

Available July 2004